Acknowledgement

My dear cousin Scottie Scott who provided many insights and gave a fresh, realistic perspective

My editor Ashley Ratcliff, who helped me craft my thoughts into this beautiful work of my life story and for staying beside me for the long haul. We did it.

My long time friend D. D.

My film instructor, Charlie Powell, for encouraging me to put my story on paper and believing in me

To the people in my life who help make this possible (you know who you are)

This letter is intended to highly recommend Tweetie Bond's new book, entitled "I'm Baby Girl and This Is My Story."

As an Emmy Award-winning film and video producer/director with more than 25 years in the business, I have seldom read a book with more raw emotion and drama as "Baby Girl." Based on a true story of Tweetie Bond growing up in a tough Detroit neighborhood, it examines Tweetie Bond's life from a pampered daughter of two famous and highly talented parents, to her descent into drugs, prostitution, abuse and prison. Along the way, she runs across many infamous people in the black community, which sends her life into an unfortunate direction. After she stumbles into hell, she fights long and hard and somehow manages to come out of it stronger and more resilient than ever.

I give Tweetie Bond my highest recommendation for having the courage to overcome her personal tragedies and explode out the other end with this wonderful, heartfelt book. I encourage you to help her promote her new book as a means of helping other troubled women in the African-American community.

By the way, Tweetie Bond is also multi-talented. She recently starred in a soon to be released film entitled "Cell Phone Genie." In the film, she played an out of control, evil hairdresser who tries to steal the genie. What she really steals is the show because she is so unbelievably good.

Look out world. Here comes Tweetie Bond!

Sincerely,

Charles Powell
Producer/Director
Powell Productions
2600 W 225th St
Torrance, CA 90505
310-880-6427

I'M
Baby Girl
AND
THIS IS MY STORY

Tweetie Bond

Order this book online at www.trafford.com
or email orders@trafford.com

Most Trafford titles are also available at major online book retailers.

Printed in the United States of America.

ISBN: 978-1-4269-5956-1 (sc)
ISBN: 978-1-4269-5955-4 (hc)
ISBN: 978-1-4269-5957-8 (e)

Library of Congress Control Number: 2011903460

Trafford rev. 04/19/2011

 www.trafford.com

North America & international
toll-free: 1 888 232 4444 (USA & Canada)
phone: 250 383 6864 ♦ fax: 812 355 4082

Contents

Introduction

If she had known back then what she knows now, she would have suffered less from the poor decisions she made. But this is the hand that was dealt to Baby Girl. Cursing like a sailor, having parents who verbally abused each other, being free to do whatever she wanted and living with family friends who molested her – these were all things that were normal to young Baby Girl. As she grew older, she went from being the apple of her father's eye to being the object of desire of many pimps and drug dealers. Without her mother's guidance – a casualty that came along with her parents' divorce – this lifestyle soon led Baby Girl down the path of destruction. Eventually, she dabbled in prostitution, smuggling drugs for her kingpin boyfriend and boosting – she got caught up in the fast life in the inner city of Detroit, Michigan, which led to numerous jail sentences and then prison. The criminal lifestyles of Baby Girl and her abusive husband infected and affected her sons. After several misjudgments and painful experiences, Baby Girl is still standing. What seems like a life destined for disaster has become a well of new hope and enlightenment.

CHAPTER 1:

The Quiet Before the Storm

Sitting in the sunshine of her innocence,
unaware of the turbulence to come.

"Bitch, you must think I'm crazy. Talkin' nat shit about tha nigga keep lookin' at chew. Ha in tha fuck you know he lookin' if you ain't lookin' at him?"

"Nigga, please. Here you come with that same ol' shit."

"Naw, bitch. Here you come."

"Naw, nigga. You da bitch. You know every hoe in the club. You fuckin' talk shit to all of 'em, and you got the black gall to start some shit wit me. Niggas and flies – two things I despise."

"Ain't that a bitch?"

"Your problem is, you a stupid muthafucka. I done set around here and made babies with a stupid muthafucka."

"Stupid muthafucka? You callin' me a stupid muthafucka? Naw, it's you and yoe white mammy dat's stupid muthafuckas."

"Why you black Alabama porch monkey. I ain't said shit 'bout that bucket-head bitch you call yoe mama."

"Aw, bitch. Eat some shit and die … You arrogant, simple muthafucka."

"You think you look good, don't chew? Fuck with me, nigga, and you'll look gruesome."

"Fuck you, bitch."

"Fuck you, nigga."

"Fuck you and tha gray hairs on yoe white mammy's pussy."

"Fuck you and yoe punk-ass mammy."

"Fuck you."

"Fuck you!"

They were squaring off – Mom with a skillet, Dad with a chair and both clenching knives with angry, stressed hands – then, in comes Baby Girl and her little sister. Baby Girl took her place at the front door, and Sugar went in the room where her parents were.

Now, the sisters – with all the urgency they could muster and like a scene from a horror movie – kick in with nonstop, deafening screams. No words, just screams. Loud screams as if for life itself. Then, as if that didn't get Mom and Dad's attention, the little one would break into an ear-splitting, glass-shattering squeal that would make Ella Fitzgerald proud, as well as wake up the entire neighborhood. This method worked every time.

One might think that was an end-of-life-as-we-know-it argument. On the contrary, this was commonplace at the Beatty household, where Mom was drop-dead gorgeous and Dad was extremely handsome. Both were entertainers and party animals who, even after marriage, continued to find the opposite sex irresistible. Neither had clean hands.

Putting that fact aside, one can surmise that the Beattys were in a very tumultuous union, but when it came to matters of the children, these homeowners were there at the 150-percent level. The Beatty kids – Baby Girl, Sugar and Tom – had to attend Sunday school and church every week, and couldn't miss any days of school. Mother-daughter and father-son heart-to-heart conversations and advice flowed freely, and, materially, the children did not want for anything. Even to this day, the Beattys quote their parents.

Life is a beautiful yet peculiar thing. It's funny how certain changes in your set of circumstances can set the tone for your future.

I'm Baby Girl and this is my story.

At about 2 years of age, I started to become aware of life and the effects I had on it, through words like: "What pretty, curly hair you have"; "Stop it"; "Put that down"; "Aw, shit, Baby Girl"; "Touch it and I'ma whip yoe little ass"; "Sulene, look what Baby Girl did"; "Take that shit out of your mouth"; and "You want a whippin', don't you?" Then, as time passed, I began to understand the big picture. I understood that I was my father's pet, pride and joy; that I was special and gifted and could do no wrong; that I had the prettiest, curly hair in the world and could do anything I wanted. Named after my father's mother and grandmother, my dad told me that it was

OK for me to cuss if I wanted to. I was without a doubt my father's anointed one. Oh, and did I say I was in charge of everything?

So we find Baby Girl playing hopscotch, jacks, jump rope and hide-and-go-seek with her new friend, Stella. Her brother, Tom, was off putting a sheet around his neck, then jumping of the porch and saying with conviction, "Superman!" Life was normal!

When my little sister, Sugar, was born, I was so excited 'cause she was my baby, too. I remember my mother, father, baby sister and older brother lived in this three-bedroom house on the North end of Detroit. I also had an eight-year-older brother, JB, and a nine-year-older sister, Tulum, who both lived down south with my mother's mother. My little sister and I slept in the same bed until we got twin beds later. We started with humble beginnings, but we were surrounded by love and were exposed to a wide range of individuals through music.

Music was a big part of my life, as my parents were well-known musicians. My mother, Sulene Beatty, also was an actress and once was offered a part in a Hollywood movie. She played piano. My father was known in the jazz world as "the Great Joe Beatty," and he, too, played the piano. He dressed sharp, and had the personality to match his pretty red and black car. Rosa Parks, Dinah Washington and Billie Holiday were some of my parents' friends. With seven aunts and four uncles, family gatherings at Christmas were filled with warmth, laughter, joy – and liquor.

The trips to Alabama to visit Grandma were not so pleasant, with the red mud, clay, dirt or whatever, stifling heat, no sidewalks, hog feedings and the worst thing imaginable – outhouse toilets. Did I say they had outhouse toilets? But I learned early in life that with happy times come trying times.

Once, when my little sister was about 6 months old, my mother and her friend, Ella, had put Sugar and me to bed, and they went up the street to have a drink. A short time later, Ella thought about us and told my mother that she was going back to check on Baby Girl and Sugar.

When Ella walked in and looked at Sugar, she turned and ran as fast as she could back to the bar and told my mother that my little sister had turned blue. The two of them ran back to the house and called the ambulance, which rushed Sugar to the hospital. Sugar had swallowed an open safety pin. They kept her in the hospital about seven months. When Sugar finally came home, I was so happy because she was my only baby sister. I treated her like she was my very own baby doll. Sugar had gotten a hold of the safety pin in my little rag doll that she was playing with. When Sugar came home from the hospital, I made sure I took good care of her. I would comb her hair, put water and grease in it, then roll it up with my fingers and make her Shirley Temple curls all over her head. Sugar looked just like Shirley Temple.

On a humorous note, once my mother and her brother had been drinking after a cousin had died. They planned to attend the funeral, but they started drinking long before it was time for the service. They took me with them to the funeral (I was about 5 or 6), and as we approached the casket, they were crying and sobbing, only to get to the casket and find out that lying inside was a person they had never seen before. They were at the wrong funeral. They dried up and quickly and quietly left to find their real cousin.

Another fond memory I have is holding my mother's hand as she took me to my first day of school. I was so excited, as I had really looked forward to that day, but I was somewhat afraid and started to cry upon finding out that my mother would not stay with me. I cried uncontrollably for a half hour or so. After a while, I settled down and began to notice my surroundings. I remember my kindergarten teacher, Mrs. Bell, who was a white lady. She was very nice and kind and I really liked her. When my mother picked me up at the end of the day, I told her how much I liked school. I liked home, too.

My mother would take me with her whenever she went shopping. We would catch the bus and go to a place called the Eastern Market, where we would buy food on an area called Russell and Gratiot. We would also go to the 5- and 10-cent store and the Goodwill store.

My father always took me with him to pay the mortgage, somewhere in Highland Park on Woodard Street. I had so much fun with my mother and dad.

One day my brother, Tom, went to the mailbox, climbed up on the banister and fell over to the ground. He fractured his skull. He was rushed to the hospital and nearly died.

Then my mother gave birth to my brother, David, and life couldn't get much better for me. So good was life for me that I alone was given the key to the trunk in my parents' bedroom, where my father kept his money. Kids in the neighborhood always said I was so lucky to have a father who gave me money whenever I wanted it. In truth, I was taking the money without asking. I soon was caught by my dad when I decided to take two dollars, instead of the change that I usually took. After my impeachment, my key was taken. My dad then gave that prize to my little sister. I was down but nowhere near out, because I knew my dad would not and could never stay upset with me. I wish that was the case with my mother.

The day my mother and father separated was the saddest day of my life. Now, considering all the menacing arguments they seemed to always have, who knows how long they would have been together? But as a child, I thought I'd done something wrong and caused them to split up. I always thought my mother and baby brother would come back home.

On that sad day that everything came crashing down, my dad went out Saturday night to play piano with his band. I saw my dad on TV and then went to bed. Later that night or early in the morning, my father didn't have or couldn't find his house key, so he knocked on the window to wake me up, saying, "Baby Girl, open the door for Daddy." Half asleep, I went and opened the door for him. He came in and turned on the lights, and we saw my mother on the couch half undressed and a man on the floor with his penis sticking out of his pants. They had been drinking and had fallen asleep. My dad said very sternly, "Baby Girl, go to bed." I did.

When I woke up the next morning, my mother had two black eyes and then my father told me that my mother had to leave. He took her and my baby brother to the Greyhound bus station and sent them to Cleveland, Ohio, where her sister lived. I cried because I didn't want my mother to leave. I was 7 years old, Tom was 8 years old and Sugar was 4 years old. So we stayed at the house with my father for about three months with no mother. When he first sent my mother away, I cried really hard and my father told me, "Baby Girl, don't cry. I'm going to buy you a white Cadillac and a white poodle dog, and I'm going to get a white woman." I was speechless because I didn't know if there was anything he could say to help the situation.

Then my father rented out our upstairs to my uncle, Jake. In reality, Jake was not an uncle but actually my mother's cousin, but he was old enough to be an uncle. I said, "I don't want to call you Cousin Jake, so can I call you Uncle Jake?" He said that was OK. Then everyone in the family started calling him Uncle Jake. He had a 12-barrel corn whiskey still for about three years, until the police busted our house. This was in the 1950s. When they poured out all of the whiskey – rolling it around to the front of our house, way down the street in the neighborhood – it smelled really bad. The police were getting ready to take my father to jail and he whispered to me to start crying and begging the police to please not lock him up. So I got down on my knees and started sobbing. I said, "Please, mister police. Don't take my daddy to jail." When my dad came walking down the street the next morning, I was happy to see him.

My daddy sold corn liquor that he made in the upstairs apartment we had at our house. My sister would sit on the counter with her little night gown pouring shots of liquor – and quoting passages from the Bible about their evil ways – for the patrons at my dad's after-hours spot. Her sermons would leave some of them crying. This was all normal in my world.

Soon, my father let his friend, Tim, move in with us and he molested me. He put me on his lap and stuck his fingers up in my private part. He did this five or six times, and I was only 6 years old. Mr. Tim was a very good cook, but my father's concern was his three children eating every day while he was at work. He didn't know what Mr. Tim was doing to me. One day, we got in the back seat of my father's car, while he and Mr. Tim sat in the front with my father driving and me in the back seat. My father always had a new car. Out of the clear blue he said, "Tim, if I ever found out that you touched one of my kids, nigger I'd kill you." Mr. Tim became nervous when my dad said that. He said, "Joe Beatty, I would never do anything like that." I was in the back seat very scared after that, but Mr. Tim didn't touch me anymore. I never told my father because I knew my father would kill him, and I didn't want him to end up going to jail. That would mean I couldn't see him anymore.

So we were living on McLean for ages. I was around 7 and my father had some tenants living upstairs. Mr. Ed and Mrs. C had three boys and a girl. Mr. Ed molested all of his children so Mrs. C would look after Sugar, Tom and I while my dad was at work. Mrs. C would cook, although she really didn't know how. Her husband, Mr. Ed, molested me and tried to molest Sugar. He would always pull out a quarter, put it in his ear and that meant he was going to get me, and I was so scared. I was afraid to tell my dad that he would play with me with his fingers and pulled his penis out six or seven times. He would have me in our bathroom but he never tried to expose himself to me. Later on in my life, Mr. Ed's son, Mitch, grew up and tried to molest my son, Carlos, as well as all of his own sister's children and his girlfriend's children. One of his other sons called Professor eventually killed somebody and wound up in jail for life.

Sometimes giving a child the right or expressing an attitude that he or she can do anything they want can backfire on you, as was the case when I was on punishment for lying and my father told me that I could not go to Cleveland to visit my mother. This so upset me that while my dad went to drop my sister and brother, JB, at Uncle Jake's for the trip to Ohio. I went into his coat pocket and took $40 – enough money for me, 10, and Tom, 11, to act out my plan. The grand scheme involved taking a taxi to the bus station, and once there, I befriended an older woman and told her a somewhat enhanced sob story that my mother left us in Detroit and that we were just trying to visit her. I asked the lady if she could please help us, to which she replied, "Sure, baby." The kind woman then bought me and Tom tickets with the money I gave her, and just like that we youngsters were off to Cleveland. When we arrived in the city, me and Tom caught a cab to our mother's house with the change. We even made it in before Uncle Jake and the others got there.

When I returned to Detroit to face the music with my father, all he said was, "I went to the credit union and got $50. I bet you won't get this, you little rogue. You'll steal anything that ain't nailed down."

About three months later, here comes this white woman, Ms. Dottie, my dad's new girlfriend. Three months before she came, I was doing an excellent job of taking care of my younger siblings. I did the laundry. I fed them delicious meals of hot dogs with pork and beans, I'll admit that once, my father cursed me for ruining his white T-shirts by putting my red pants in with them. Now Ms. Dottie wanted to take over what I was doing. I was so pissed off. Who needed her anyway? I knew what I was doing. I could boil clothes and wash hot dogs with the best of them. So you can see why I hated her, which is probably why she didn't care too much for me. But she liked Sugar and Tom.

Ms. Dottie would sit and roll cigarettes and have her first cousin come over every day and drink corn whiskey with her. He never came on weekends though, because my father was home. My father worked afternoons at Chrysler from 3 p.m. to midnight and Ms. Dottie would be sitting at the kitchen table, and right before my father pulled up in his car after getting off work, she would run to the bedroom and get into bed.

I was going to Washington Elementary School, and the constant teasing from the other kids made me embarrassed that Ms. Dottie was my stepmother. I hated that. One day, I got kicked out of school and my father said Ms. Dottie was going to take me back to school. I said to him that I was not going back to school if she was taking me. So he took me back. Sugar and Tom called her Mama Dottie, but I called her Ms. Dottie. I really didn't like her and she really didn't like me. On a Saturday when my father was home, Ms. Dottie demanded that I mop the living room floor.

I said, "OK," and went to get the mop, at which point she screeched, "Put it back. You're going to get down on your hands and knees to clean this floor."

I listened, even though I had never gotten down on the floor to mop in my entire life. Ms. Dottie then told me to take the toothbrush she had in her hand and use it instead to scrub the floor. As I'm doing as I'm told, she threw down some rice on the floor behind me so that when I backed up while scrubbing, the rice stuck into my knees. That is a special kind of pain I'll never forget.

I'd had enough. Rising up from the cold, hard tile, I let her have a piece of my mind.

"I'm not gonna mop anything else. You can't make me."

"OK then. Let's see what your father has to say about that, young lady."

"Go on. Tell him, 'cause I'm not doin' this no more."

Calling my bluff, she went in the room and woke up my daddy and told him exactly what I just said. I wasn't scared though. See, I was the apple of my father's eye, and he would never let this woman get away with treating me like garbage.

My father got up, came into the living room and said, "Baby Girl, you are not minding Dottie."

But when I told him what she did, he asked her why she would do such a mean thing. Ms. Dottie said it was all because I was bad.

Within a moment, Daddy had reached a verdict, and I won that battle, as I'd hoped.

"Get up off that floor. Dottie, you clean up this mess."

I wish I could say that this incident put to rest the awkward tension between us, but Ms. Dottie's disdain for me was like a priority on her daily to-do list. It seemed never-ending. Maybe a few weeks later, she cooked a mouth-watering meal of neck bones and black-eyed peas for my sister and brother, while she served me – the second-class problem child – duck blood soup with some white potatoes. What an awful treat that was when we all came to the dinner table to eat. Outrage set in upon looking at that slop on my plate.

I couldn't help but ask, "What in the hell is this you're feeding me?"

She replied, "Duck blood soup. Sugar and Tom get to eat the good stuff because they know how to behave. Since you don't, you get what you get."

"Well, I'm not eatin' that shit," I retorted.

I stormed out of the house and went to my girlfriend's place. I then called Uncle Jake and his wife, Aunt Susie, and told them what was happening. They lived about 15 minutes away and hurried over.

When my aunt and uncle arrived, Ms. Dottie had put on the same song and dance she gave my dad a few weeks beforehand.

"Baby Girl likes to curse me out whenever I tell her to do something," Dottie told them. "That's her punishment for acting out."

"You listen here, heifer. You better not ever try and feed that girl some shit like that again," Uncle Jake shouted.

Later, I found out that duck blood soup was a regular part of the Polish diet, but I didn't know that then.

When things had calmed down a few months later, Ms. Dottie bought me a bicycle that I really wanted. I had to work hard for that bike, too. I had to promise her I would be good. Just as soon as she had given me that gift – a shiny, baby blue dream fit for a princess – she let her anger get the best of her when I did something she didn't like. Ms. Dottie, without hesitating, gave my bike to my brother Tom. I was really mad and decided I was going to make sure he didn't get it.

One Saturday, my mother was coming to see us from where she lived with her sister in Cleveland. Ms. Dottie and my father went to the Greyhound bus station to pick her up. Ms. Dottie was scared shitless to go with him because my mother was coming to stay for a few days with us because we missed her and wanted to see her. My mom slept in the room with me and my sister. Imagine the fear Ms. Dottie had knowing that her boyfriend's ex-wife was sleeping a few doors down, as she lay with him.

Now when they pulled up in front of the house, Tom and I had just had a very, very serious altercation that started and ended like this: There were about six or seven pop bottles worth 5 cents each. As I was getting ready to cash them in at the corner store, my brother stepped up and said, "You can't take these – they my bottles," and snatched them out of my hands. Then I snatched them from him and said, "No, they not. These my muthafuckin' bottles." At this point, the bottles were everywhere. I was so pissed off that I took three bottles and went to the back of the house, where Tom had his new bike, took aim, threw the bottles broke some of the spokes from the tire rim. Next, he jumped on me, threw me down and started choking me so hard that I could hardly breathe. When I got up, I knew the solution was not to play Popeye and pop a can of spinach, so I went and got the butcher knife. He was at the bottom of the front steps, when I yelled at him, "Muthafucka, I'ma kill yoe ass for choking me. Now come up one step and see don't I do it."

"All right then," he said, acting bold and taking a step up.

Then I said, "Come up one more step. I dare you."

We repeated this a couple more times until Tom was just a few feet away from me. Then, I snapped. I threw the knife and it landed in his appendix. When I saw him there with the blade in him, I ran and grabbed him, feeling an instant remorse. What was I thinking?

"I'm so sorry," I cried out, desperate for some sign that my brother would be fine.

He uttered a pained, "You done killed me; I'm going to die."

I laid my head in his chest and pleaded, "No, Tom. Don't die!"

Just then, panic set in as I looked up and saw the car pull up with my father and Ms. Dottie riding in the front and my mother in the back. My father ran up the stairs, picked Tom up, put him in the car and rushed him to the hospital. My mother saw all of this and took me into the backyard, got a switch off the tree and started whipping me. I was so mad that I bit her on the thigh. That sure enough stopped the whipping. This was not the grand homecoming that I had envisioned for my mother.

When my father returned from the hospital, he said the doctors decided to keep my brother there for two days. Tom came home and received the royal treatment. They even brought him lunch in bed. I was nervous about what he would say to me, but I couldn't let on how awful I was really feeling. So I went into his room to visit him and sat on the edge of his bed.

"How are you doing?" I asked my bandaged brother.

"I'm OK now. It still hurts a little, though."

Now, this could have been a tender moment for us two to make amends, but my mannish self blurted out, "I bet you won't fuck with me no mo'."

"Daddy, Daddy, come here," Tom yelled out.

My brother told on me as soon as our father hurriedly stepped through that doorway.

"Get yoe little fast ass out of his bedroom now. And I bet' not catch you saying nothing like that again," Daddy warned me.

I would take the verbal scolding over the physical one mother had given me earlier, although I probably deserved another spanking.

When the time came for my mother to go back to Cleveland and leave us again with Ms. Dottie, I didn't want her to leave but she had to go. That Monday at school, word had spread fast about the knife situation. All the kids started calling me Jack the Ripper on the way home. Never one to take no mess from no one, I cursed them out, just like my daddy told me to.

"They talk mess; you talk it right back louder," Father would say. "They hit you; you hit back harder."

It goes without saying that I came from a very dysfunctional family. And the major contributor of that dysfunction was at it again, several months later. I don't recall exactly what set Ms. Dottie off this time, but apparently I did something to really aggravate her, so much so that she took a pair of shears to my favorite skirt.

One evening, I placed it on the ironing board to bump it out to wear to school the next day. When I was finished, I turned the iron off, left the skirt on the board and went outside to play. When I got back inside, what used to be my cute, pleated skirt was sliced to shreds. I couldn't understand for the life of me why Ms. Dottie would do something so harsh me, especially when I didn't do anything wrong. Believe me, when I saw what she did, I got mad and went into her closet and cut up about 10 pieces of her clothes. She didn't tell my father when I did this because she knew he would find out what she did to me first. He says that I had to respect Ms. Dottie. But that lady did not like me. She never combed my hair, only my sister's hair. She never talked to me about life, boys or anything else. She did wash the clothes and cook. That was it.

You could say, however, that Ms. Dottie was a busy woman. One time, she cheated on my father and I caught her. Normally, every single day, she would be sitting at the kitchen table when I came home from school, about 3:15 in the afternoon. So, one Friday, I came home from school and there was no Ms. Dottie sitting at the kitchen table. I got home, went into my bedroom and heard some noise coming from upstairs in our two story house, from an area in the back. I heard the bed up there rocking. I stood up on my dresser to get a closer listen to the noise through the ceiling. That vulgar melody was Ms. Dottie and some man having sex. When I heard them both walking down the steps, I ran to the front of the house to see who he was. His car was out front and it was a black '59 Buick. After getting a good glimpse, I ran back into the kitchen. Ms. Dottie then walked in the back door with a guilty look on her face.

"Where have you been, Ms. Dottie? You wudn't in yoe chair when I got home," I asked already knowing the answer.

"Oh, I was just up the street at Ms. Lucy's house."

"You're telling a lie; you were upstairs doing the pussy with Mr. Frank."

"I was not. How dare you make up an awful story like that about me?"

"Yes you were," I taunted back at Ms. Dottie. "I got on top of my dresser and heard you and him doing the pussy. I'm gonna to tell my daddy."

She was anxious that whole evening and sent my brother to the store to buy us some ice cream, as if that was enough to erase that very vivid memory. I helped myself to a nice, big bowl of chocolate ice cream, and as Ms. Dottie paced back and forth across the kitchen, I told her, "I'm still telling my dad."

Still, she sent Tom back to the store two more times to buy us all ice cream. She had never in her life brought me a sweet reward; she'd only bought it for my little sister and brother. So, after the third ice cream, I told her I was still letting my dad know what happened. Ms. Dottie turned cherry tomato red, as the anticipation of Daddy's arrival grew more intense. That night, I stayed up and waited for my father to get off work. He came home and she was still sitting at the kitchen table, smoking cigarettes like crazy. Before he could ask me what I was doing up so late, I greeted him with, "Guess what. Today when I came home from school, Ms. Dottie was upstairs with Mr. Frank doing the pussy."

Ms. Dottie's face was covered in tears. That was confirmation enough, but my father asked, "Is that true what Baby Girl said?"

She wouldn't reply. She wouldn't say anything one way or the other.

"Baby Girl, kick her ass."

Can you imagine, my father telling me to beat up my stepmother and I'm only 9 years old?

"My pleasure," I thought.

I grabbed her, threw her down on the floor and started punching her in the face and head. When he felt content with the damage I had done, my father grabbed me up off her.

"That's enough, Baby Girl."

At that point, I went to bed, my heart still racing and mind imagining what would come next.

Ms. Dottie really hated me now. I don't know what she did but she was locked up for 60 days in Macomb County Jail in Clinton Township, Michigan. I never found out what she did, but I sure was glad she had left. So, we were home alone again when we get out of school because my dad works the afternoon shift. For two months, I was back in charge of my sister and brother, and we managed just fine. Ms. Dottie came home from jail and moved back to our house. Of course, my father was very happy she was home. I wasn't.

She knew some private investigator named Mr. Minor. I don't know what she told him, but he seemed to think that my father was engaging in inappropriate activity with me. I want to tell the world that I was my father's pet. He named me after his mother, and my father never in his life, ever approached me in that way. My father wasn't that kind of man, period. This private investigator took me to his apartment downtown one day and gave me candy, cookies and ice cream. Mr. Minor said he had to talk to me about some things that were really important. He proceeded to ask me if my father had ever touched me in my private area. Boy, did I get upset!

"My daddy ain't never done nothing like that at all. I don't want to talk any more. Take me back home," I demanded.

I missed a day from school because of the ill-intentioned interrogation at Mr. Minor's apartment. I don't know what the deal was, and I don't know if Ms. Dottie was going with Mr. Minor or not, but that was the last time I saw him. When my father came home, I told him everything that was said and done. He was very angry with Ms. Dottie for going behind his back and telling that man that she suspected stuff about my daddy and me. All this because she didn't like me.

Surprisingly, Ms. Dottie still was with my father a few years later, when I was about 12 years old. But her ways hadn't changed. Ms. Dottie was cheating with a black man who lived on the next street up from us. Wilson was his name, and he sold corn whiskey. Another Friday night went by that she didn't come home because she spent the night at Wilson's house. My dad came home from work that night and Ms. Dottie wasn't at home. He asked me where she was, but I didn't know. Then, I started wondering where she could be and pondered myself to sleep.

The next day, my father left and was gone all day. I was thinking and thinking about where Ms. Dottie could be. I know Mr. Wilson lives on the next block over and sells corn whiskey, which was her favorite to drink. So following an idea, I went over to his house to look for her. I knocked on his door, and he wasn't expecting me, although he knows my father and knows who I am. I asked if he had seen Ms. Dottie, and he told me he hadn't, but when he opened the door I saw her sitting in the chair in the kitchen. My blood started to boil at this sight, but I just headed back home. I packed up all her clothes, spreading her yellow wool coat out in the floor to use as the wrapper. Next, I grabbed a rope that was part of the clothes line and tried to tie it up but couldn't lift it. So, I dragged it to the porch and rolled it down the steps to the ground. Then, I went back to Mr. Wilson's house and knocked on the door.

He opened the door and said, "Little girl, I told you Dottie wasn't here."

"Yes, she is here because I saw her in your kitchen. You tell Ms. Dottie her clothes are on the sidewalk in front of my house and if she wants them, she better come and get them." The next thing I know, Mr. Wilson drove her to my house and got her clothes. I guess that meant she was moving in with him.

I eagerly await my father's arrival home. I had some good news to share.

"Daddy, Daddy, guess what," I said to my father, who looked at me with a curious smile. "I just put Ms. Dottie out."

As the grin left his face, he asked, "How you gonna put my woman out?"

"I didn't think you'd want her any more, after she had spent the night with Mr. Wilson." Instead of hearing, "Job well done, Baby Girl," Dad shouted, "Get out."

I was saddened because of his reaction, but on the other hand, I was glad because Ms. Dottie never came back to our house again. Now we're alone and a few months later, my mother Sulene moved back with us from Cleveland into the house on McLean Street. She and my father were not getting along at all. They bickered about bills, disciplining us kids, and who was contributing more to keep the family afloat. My father moved to the upstairs apartment in our house because they couldn't be civil with each other.

In the amusement park called life, I was preparing to get on the roller coaster.

CHAPTER 2:

The Dismantling of Baby Girl

Mental torture and physical violence in most cases leaves you with no self-esteem.

Life has its brighter side. On a lighter note, once, when visiting my grandmother in Alabama, a very funny thing happened to my older brother, JB – the brother who successfully escaped every attempt I made to control and take him over, which really pissed me off. So, consequently, we had our run-ins, but on this occasion, I felt sorry for him. For it appeared that not just one, but a whole hive of bumblebees stung him on his top lip, and it had swollen to the point that it looked like a two-nosed, one-lipped alien. My poor brother was in so much pain that he had to lie down and somehow deal with it.

When I told my grandmother, who honestly and truly believed that she, ordained by God, had the ability to heal – which she delivered with a resounding and firm healing smack on the affected area – she set out to relieve JB's misery with a healing. After seeing how big his lip had swollen, Grandma had no choice. Lying asleep face up on his bed, concentrating or maybe unconscious, he didn't know he was about to be healed. Grandma said a prayer and then gave him one of those resounding and firm healing smacks on his bumblebee juice-filled lip. My brother hollered out loud – in this Christian household, this healing house of prayer, my grandmother's temple – the very first cuss word he ever spoke in Grandma's house: "Goddamit, Ma! Leave me alone!" I could not stop laughing, mainly because the smack didn't heal him, at least not as much as it hurt him.

The Detroit inner city in the '60s and '70s glorified the hustlers and pimps. They had the lifestyle of entertainers, flamboyant and seemingly rich. They did not have regular jobs. They had personality and could sweet talk you – by that I mean "talk shit," "con your socks off you," and did I say they could and would terrorize and frighten the hell out of you?

In the mid-1960s, Robert Beck, also known as Iceberg Slim, wrote a book called "Pimp: The Story of My Life." It was a big hit in most inner cities across the United States and caused, it seems, every Negro and his momma to want to be a pimp. Iceberg actually was a role model for a lot of young black men in Detroit. It was a "how to be a pimp" book with guidelines to keep you on the beaten path. In this climate, there was not much for a girl to choose from. Plus, working people don't party like fast-life people.

Me and my friends, who used to play with dolls and mud pies, when we grew into teenagers, would talk about getting money through crime. I was not poor like some of my friends and not desperate for money. I always had money, so they didn't include me in their hardcore crime plots. Most of the things they felt were way over my head. It seemed that I wasn't cut out for the violent criminal acts my friends were planning. Having to face the world without my mother's guidance would eventually present one problem after another for me.

When I was in the eighth grade at Cleveland Junior High School, my brother Tom and I were in the same homeroom and social studies class, which meant that I was there to keep him in line, but at the same time watch after him. I still defended him.

One day, our social studies teacher, Mr. Johns, asked Tom a question he didn't know the answer to. That wasn't good enough for our demanding instructor, who hid his Captain Hook hand from the students. So Mr. Johns walked over to Tom and slapped him back and forth with his good hand. I was sitting over in the next row and saw this, and went into shock. My dad said long ago that I could cuss when and if I wanted to, so I was on automatic pilot when I screamed, "Muthafucka, you don't slap my brother." The teacher came chasing after me like a scene out taken from a "Little Rascals" movie. I started to run from my seat around chairs and tables. I picked up a thick textbook and threw it at him, striking his right arm. Even more incensed by this attack, Mr. Johns continued his pursuit, so I ran around some more chairs, hurled the globe and got him good on the forehead. Still, as he chased after me, I picked up a juice glass filled with pencils on his desk. This time, with Mr. Johns unable or unwilling to duck, the cup smacked him on his lips and he finally had caught me. The flustered teacher took out that hooked hand and stuck it in my neck to try to hold me. But he couldn't subdue me for long. I broke loose from his grip and ran out of the classroom.

Hearing the commotion, the other teachers came and took me to the office. It wasn't until I was sitting in the principal's office that I noticed that my neck was bleeding, as a result of Mr. Johns' assault. The administrators told me I was expelled and needed to call my dad before he left for work. Within minutes of me placing that frantic phone call, explaining why I'd acted out, my father stormed into the school and he wanted answers.

"Where's the motherfucker that stuck his hook hand in my daughter's neck?"

Trying to protect that monster of a teacher, one of the office ladies said, "Mr. Beatty, he is gone for the day."

"He's not gone, and when I find him, I'm going to kick his ass. Nobody ever lays a hand on my daughter and gets away with it," Dad retorted.

After seeing all this, when I reminded my father that they wanted to kick me out of school, the principal said that I could return to school the next day.

I was a handful for my father at times, but my falling in love at the age of 13 with one of the guys from around the way would prove to be a whole other set of problems, for my dad and for myself.

His name was Poppa Swotty, and he was so smooth. I was sitting on the front porch at a friend's house, when he approached me as he was walking by. He was charming but a lot older than my friends and me. He had completed a tour of duty in the Army – and had been dishonorably discharged – while none of my friends were old enough to join. He was by far more aggressive than any of my friends. It made me feel so special that this 19-year-old big shot would even find me – a naïve, plain Jane type – remotely attractive. After coming around the block to see me a few times, Poppa Swotty said he wanted to make me his, and I was glad to finally have a boyfriend.

But when we started dating, my father could not stand him. One day, Daddy saw the two of us holding hands, as Poppa Swotty was walking me home. My father was so upset at this outward display of affection that he told him, "You better not walk across my sidewalk again."

It was shortly after that that my dad started to show signs of mental frailty. It was a sad time for me as I watched my once proud, outgoing and still outspoken father deteriorate. Once at a restaurant, he shouted out to a waitress, "You hamburger-hustlin' muthafucka!" Me and my sister could only look at each other, and I knew she was thinking what I was thinking: "What the hell is happening to Dad?" On another occasion, he, while in court, had begun to address the charge of why he hit this lady with his cane. Drifting away from the issue, he loudly began to state that he was a soldier who fought for his country. Then reiterating that he was a veteran and after again being asked to address the allegations, Dad said to the judge, "Aw, man. Every nigga in Hamtramck been in that bitch." Somehow, being a veteran helped my father out of this situation. My sister and I were embarrassed, to say the least. This was not the dad we knew.

On my father's dying bed at Eloise Hospital, my dad, who at age 55 suffered a heart attack, uttered his last words to me: "Baby Girl, you leave that nigger."

It wasn't that easy, though. At 16, I was in love. Poppa Swotty gave me butterflies, and for the first time in my life made me feel like a woman. Without having my mother in the house to tell me about boys, I didn't have a standard to strive for. I did everything my boyfriend told me to do because I was really scared of him or what he would do to me if I made him unhappy. At this point, I was wondering what I had gotten myself into. Little did I know, Poppa Swotty was a pimp, and an insanely jealous pimp at that.

Poppa Swotty really loved me, too, but he had a funny way of showing it. He beat me every day for nothing. I remember the first episode happened only three or four months into the relationship. I was at my girlfriend, Marsha's house, watching TV in her room. She lived with her brother and grandparents and was a tomboy, not a lesbian. I never entertained the thought of sex with any woman. I was still going to my girlfriends' house to play. We still had dolls. At this point in my life, I've spent more time as a child than anything else. I had my first sexual encounter with Poppa Swotty only a month ago, but he was older and thought differently, more like an adult. I was too young to know who I was. Let Poppa Swotty tell it, we were messing around. He had been looking for me that afternoon, and when he found out where I was, he came over to Marsha's house and jabbed a wire hanger into my thigh, accusing me of misdeeds with Marsha. I bled everywhere, but I couldn't let anyone in my family know what he'd done to me. At this point in my life, I thought this was the way men were supposed to treat women.

I remember neighbors who beat their wives. My parents always fought, and I beat up my stepmother for my father, so I was more than certain that men beat their women. It was normal behavior and I didn't have my mother's advice to help formulate my transition into womanhood.

If I went to the store to buy a soda, Poppa Swotty would count the change and say that I had used what was left over to call my man, which I didn't have one. For this reason, I was afraid to even say hello to another guy. We'd be walking down the street and Poppa would hit me in my eye hard enough to give me a black eye and claim I was looking at the guy who was driving down the street in a Cadillac. It was just a figment of his twisted imagination and I paid the price for his insecurities. So there I was facing life, unadvised and unsupervised, basically winging it with incorrect perceptions on what to expect from a man. Be that as it may, I am a result of my decisions, so I'm totally responsible for the rest of this story.

I was 14 years old when I ran away from home to be with Poppa Swotty. The police were looking for me, and we had nowhere to go, so we'd hang out at random people's houses and just sit and go up to the after-hours spots and just sit. Poppa Swotty was a great pool player and would beat mostly everyone he played against at the pool hall on 12th Street, where we hung out a lot. Poppa eventually got us an apartment at Seward and 12th, on the west side of Detroit.

The rent had to be paid, so he demanded that I go out and prostitute. Seeing no other way out of it, I just did as I was told, but I hated the idea of selling my body. Poppa Swotty told me what I needed to say to lure in the Johns, and just like that, I was out on the street, working for my man. My first day on the job, I was positioned on 14th Street and hitched a ride with a man. It just so happened that he was an undercover police officer. I solicited him, at which point he took out his badge and he drove me downtown to jail. I was scared out of my mind.

I stayed in juvenile hall for a month and then was sent to a place called Adrian's Girls Detention School. I was there in quarantine for 30 days, and then the administrators let me go to my own room, upstairs in the two-story house. By then, it was winter. I had one thing on my mind: getting back out into the real world with Poppa Swotty. With the paper cutting scissors they'd given us residents, I began slicing away at the window screen. It took me three days to get cut out enough of the screen to get my body out of it. I climbed up, jumped out of the second story onto the ground. I hit the ground and landed on my back, lying there immobile for about two minutes in my dress and gown. It felt like every bone in my body was broken on that rainy, foggy Tuesday night. I got up and started walking toward the highway, drenched and shivering, and hitched a ride with a white man who knew I had run away from the girls home. I asked him to take me to Detroit, which was about 90 miles away. He said he would if he could have sex with me. I was desperate and cold and scared, so I complied and he drove me to Detroit and dropped me off at the corner of my mother's house. By now, she had returned to Detroit and lived on Cody. I knocked on the door and my brother Tom answered. I was on a mission to get my clothes, change and go to my daddy's house. For some reason, I didn't trust my mother. She was just too law-abiding.

My father was so happy to see me and said I could stay there with him. Shortly afterward, my mother came around to his house. When she went inside, my parents went into the other room, where I heard her tell my father that they should call the police and turn me in. Always coming to my defense, Daddy told her she had better not call the police on his daughter. "My daughter is bad as Jessie James," he remarked, almost bragging about me. After hearing this conversation, I up and left. I hitched over to 12th Street, where I knew Poppa Swotty was at the pool room. Sure enough, there he was. He was so glad to see me, as the strain from my jump out of the window set in. My elbows were really tender, so much so that I couldn't let anything touch them. That didn't stop me, however, from wrapping my arms snugly around him. I still didn't have anywhere to stay and I really didn't care because I was back with Poppa Swotty. We hung in the after-hours club when the poolroom closed.

I quickly was brought back to reality, when Poppa wanted me to sell my body again so that we could have a place to stay because he couldn't return to stay with Beverly, his girlfriend who lived at her invalid mother's house. Three months later, I got caught again by a plain-clothes police officer, go back to juvenile hall and then Adrian's. This time, I spent three weeks in quarantine and when I was able to stay with the other girls in the house, I became fast friends with these three girls, including Nillie, and we all planned to break out. All of us in the entire dormitory were playing baseball, and we decided that once it was time to go back in we were going to run across the highway into the woods. When 3 p.m. rolled around, we carried out our plan almost too easily. We made it into the woods, which we traipsed through for about two hours. Just before dark, we came out of the woods walking down the highway trying to hitch a ride and a white man picked us up and drove us about two miles, met the police and turned us all in. Back at the girl's home, I was placed back in quarantine and had gotten poison ivy from our ill-fated fleeing attempt. While I was in quarantine, I had a visit from my mother and her friend, Mr. Wood, who set up a court hearing with my mother and discharged me, dishonorably because I kept breaking out.

I was discharged from Adrian's, and my mother had brought me home. Poppa Swotty was working in a factory for Chrysler and I had gained a lot of weight, thanks to all the buttery food at the girls' home. He wanted to marry me. I am nearly 16 years old. My mother went down to sign for me to marry him and on our wedding day at his mother and father's house I think that I am grown and drink a whole glass of vodka. I got real sick and ended up staying at my mother's house. That was our honeymoon.

As soon as he married me, he quit his job at the factory. After giving birth for the first time, love came out of me like a rainbow after the storm. I understand childbirth is a common part of the human experience, but for some reason, I felt like mine was "to the front of the line" special – damn near divine in scope, world news. My son's birth gave me more reason to live than I already had. And my second son's birth reproduced in me the same exact feeling that the first pregnancy did. Now there I was, responsible for these two lives that came out of my body. Wow. Wow. Wow. I'm the mother of two boys. Unfortunately, I couldn't apply any of the skills I obtained with my little sister. Shirley Temple curls on my boys was not going to cut it.

We were staying upstairs over my mother's house on McLean, living rent-free and Poppa Swotty was very ready for me to go out on the street and prostitute after only six weeks had passed from having the baby. I did not want to do this at all because when I was younger, I had been caught twice by the police because I didn't know what I was doing; so I was scared of going out there standing on the corner trying to catch a trick and not really knowing anything. I didn't make any money that night and when I came back home, he beat me so bad with a hanger; just like all the pimps did back in those days. This relationship was like getting accustomed to and finding comfort in hell. The next day, I went back out there again, scared and made no money. He beat me again. I think it must have come to him that I needed to be schooled by a regular prostitute, so he had a friend named Ronnie who had a woman my age who knew the ropes. She schooled me that you charge the trick $10. So I did and that night I made $20 off two tricks. I went home and he was happy. This went on for some months as Poppa Swotty started using heroin. I didn't know that he was using. The only thing I did in those days was to smoke cigarettes. So, I moved from upstairs on McLean Street back over on the west side near the 12th Street on the "ho stroll." We were living on 12th Street at the Holiday Inn Hotel on Dundee and 14th Street. It was a family hotel where we were so I met all of these working girls who lived there and we became the best of friends. There was Pat, NeNe and See See. Pat's pimp was James, NeNe's pimp was Slim Jim and See See's pimp was Tim. We girls would go on 12th street every night and work. There was a trick house and the price was $10 and $2 to Mr. Bell who ran the house. He sold wine to the whores and the tricks. I became what is called a "top money-maker," and I still was a minor. There were 15 to 20 girls working out of Mr. Bell's trick house. There were other trick houses on 12th Street. I was making so much money that Poppa Swotty's name was ringing all over the west side and Davison area where we were from. Now, they came up with some pills, which were called Seek-co's which is an upper. I started taking them because they made me brave. While I wasn't afraid anymore I didn't like men having sex with me. At first I would men put their penis between my legs and I would just hold my legs real tight but I wouldn't let their penis go inside me. I did that for so long that the tricks would complain to Mr. Bell and he barred me out of his trick house. So then I started stealing. My friends would get a trick and have him take off his pants and put them on the chair by the window. I would go in his wallet through the window and take all of his money, then put the wallet back. The trick didn't know until he got home that his wallet was empty. I was making big bank doing this. I'd also break into their cars while they were inside. I'd use a coat hanger to get in the car and take their wallet if they'd left it in the car. I'd give the girl who was upstairs with them, a little something and I was making $300 to $600 a weekend from Thursday to Saturday. I didn't work on Sunday at all. It was my day off. I got pregnant by a trick and didn't want to have a trick's baby so I had a lady perform an abortion on me. She stuck a long, skinny, red tube up me and said around the next day the baby would come out. It did as a big blood clot and it felt like it would kill me. A week went by and I was back on the stroll going into the cars, making big money. Poppa Swotty bought a Cadillac. He went and rented himself a trick house. I was really fucking up on purpose because I would come to his house and bring the trick and get the money, go to the bathroom to get water to wash 'em up but never go back to the room to deal with the trick. I would leave out of the door and go hide for a little while. Poppa Swotty was mad and very upset with me saying I couldn't do the tricks like that, but I kept doing it because I didn't like giving my body to anyone. I hated it but I had to do it for him because he was a pimp, dressed real well with everything matching and every color suit there was. I was a sharp dresser too and Poppa Swotty was jealous of me.

One day we got into it and he smashed my head into his Cadillac and dented his car. One day he came up on 12th Street to the "ho stroll" and saw me in the telephone booth. I was calling home for him and he said I was calling my man.

It got to a point where I would work when and only if I wanted to. I resisted his attempts to try to make me work every day. I knew in my mind, that shit was not for me, but now with the use of drugs being a part of our equation, his desire for me to work was to feed his habit for heroin. Things would escalate in this manner: He'd say, "Are you gonna work tonight?"

Then I'd say, "I don't feel like working."

"Ha in the fuck we gone have anything if you just gon' sit here and not do shit? You better take yoe ass out there and make me some fuckin' money, bitch."

I'd say, "I don't feel good," or anything that came out of my mouth to stop his onslaught. One time after beating my ass, he stabbed me down the middle of my forehead with an umbrella. My feeling was, "Shoot your best shot, but I'm not with this hoeing shit."

One day my girlfriend, Pat, had left her pimp, James, and choose another pimp named Bingo. Poppa kind of knew of him and was jealous of him, so we were at home one Saturday night and he accused me of having sex with Bingo. He got me and put me in the Cadillac and we drove to where Bingo was, upstairs in an after-hours joint on 12th Street. Poppy Swotty went upstairs and got Bingo and had him get in the back s eat of his car. Now, he had beaten me for about an hour with an extension cord and my back was black and welted up. He told him that he had something to tell him and then said, "This bitch says ya'll been fuckin'." Bingo says, "Baby Girl, why would you tell this man we been fuckin'?" I told him that Poppa had beat me and made me say it. Bingo turned to Poppa and told him to let him out of the car. Poppa Swotty took his gun and hit me right under my eye with the butt of the gun. They got out, and Poppa took me home saying he was sorry. There I am beaten and messed up for nothing. Another time he beat me with an extension cord and broke the lamp across my ear causing me lifelong earaches because I didn't want to go work 12th Street.

Always after his violence, he says he's sorry and wants to get romantic and have sex, which I'm not really eager for. But I'd do anything to keep him from going ape on me again.

We are living in another house and he had a friend named Unock. He was a big guy who pimped this woman named Ann. She was a very big girl prostitute. He and Poppa Swotty had become very close friends but I didn't care for either one of them. I think Unock wanted me, and one day they came over and said they were told that I'd suck Ann's pussy. That blew my mind because I never heard anything like that before. We were all in the living room and Poppa said Ann, tell Baby Girl what she did. She said, "She did suck my pussy," and I said, "You are a lie!" I never sucked anybody's pussy in my life. So, she say, yes you did. I left the living room and went into my bathroom and started crying looking in the bathroom mirror. I opened the bathroom cabinet and saw a razor blade and put it in my pocket and walked back into the living room. Very quietly, I wiped away my tears and walked over to Ann and took out the razor and cut her down her face. Poppa Swotty hit me in the mouth and knocked out my front tooth.

Poppa Swotty and I had been together for seven years, since I was 13 years old, until I was 20. I left him and moved back with my mother but he kept coming around wanting me back and I'd had my second child, Little Man who at the time was 4 months old. I didn't want to be with Poppa Swotty anymore.

But what he did to me this time was the last straw that made me see the light. This man, my husband, who loved me – I thought – had just permanently disfigured me. He knocked my fucking tooth out. This shit was over. I knew men beat their women and all, but my mind said, "Fuck this shit and fuck him, too. Life without Poppa Swotty, here I come." Now free of this relationship that had earned me a black eye for just about every major holiday in America, me and my boys would move on to greener pastures.

My mother paid for me to get my teeth fixed and he kept coming around my house.

I had moments when I started shit that could've made this man want to beat my ass, but it was our lifestyle that kept shit alive. So I felt like he started shit and I reacted to it. On more than one occasion I got sick and tired of this pimp shit, where he had to have more women and build up his stable. That didn't sit right with me. I was jealous of the other women when it came to my man. I was a hustler who would do anything for my man. I prostituted but I was not a prostitute. I did what I did hoping we – the two of us – would have a home and a brighter day. It was not my intention to make him "big daddy pimp" and his famous hoe Baby Girl, so when I saw things heading in that direction, I fought back. One time he was about to walk out the door, all dressed up on one of his pimp missions, a shit-starting, hell-raising, muthafuckin' kamikaze fool swolled up in me, causing me to up and pour a half pint of milk all over his suit and say, "See how all the bitches at The 20 Grand like you now!" I suffered no broken bones on this adventure. On another of his pimp outings, the zip damn fool in me came out again, as I seemed to have no control whatsoever, and led me to pour laundry powder on top of his newly processed hair, fuckin' up his 'do. You'd think that I was so full of fear at that point that I'd never do something so foolish as to provoke him, but I did.

We all have some fool in us – me too. I even had impromptu sex with a super fine dude while Poppa was in jail for three days.

Then, I met this real handsome guy named Butch and I let him move in my house, then found out he was shooting dope. He stayed three or four weeks before I put him out. When he left, I never saw him again. I'm trying to find me a good man, not a pimp. I met this older guy, Chad, who was a hustler and owner of an after hour joint. He was a nice man and I liked him. I stayed with him for three months until my sister, Tulum, and I and my girlfriend Mary went to a club one night. We were all sitting there in the club and Chad walked in making his rounds, which included going from club to club; where people would see him and he'd invite them to his after-hours spot. Chad walked in and saw me sitting at the bar and asked me who I was there with. I told him that it was me, my sister and Mary. He said, "OK, but if I ever catch you in another club, I'll break both your arms and legs." That did it. A light went on in my head. I was done with him. I went home after the club and stayed up until 7 a.m., when he closed the after-hours joint. Then he went home on Outer Drive where he lived in a very classy neighborhood. When he got home, I called him and told him that I didn't want to be with him anymore. All he said was, "All right, baby," and that was the end of that. I stayed by myself for a couple of months then got a job in a night club as a barmaid and I made real good money. I was stealing money, too, because Poppa Swotty's brother Lonnie was a pimp who only had white women as his prostitutes. He had the nightclub where I worked and was in partnership with this white guy. He wanted me to run the bar. They had just opened the club and I was making so much money I had my own house which I bought myself. My cousin was living with me, taking care of my boys and I didn't have a man. I was doing just great.

I really thought I was doing great. What I was doing was backing myself into a corner and digging a hole that will take me a lifetime to get out of. Watch me go down. This is the part about my life that I recommend you avoid.

CHAPTER 3:

Misguided into Darkness, Lost and Turned Out

*After having her will -- her power to resist,
broken down -- it was easy to reassemble her
into someone totally different than what she was
before.*

It's a great feeling to know that you can do things for yourself. I don't have a man, but that's perfectly fine with me. With this new-found financial freedom, I was eager to reclaim my independence, get out of my mother's house and into a place I could call my own. I had my own house, which I bought myself.

One day, when my cousin, Don, uncle Jake's son, and I went walking down the street looking for a place for rent. He suggested that we stop by the house of an old childhood friend of mine, Cherry. She and I were so close that everyone thought we were related. It had been some time since I'd seen her, so I was anxious to reconnect with her.

I later realized that his motives for linking up with Cherry were ulterior. Don was addicted to heroin and was just taking advantage of my friendship with Cherry. He knew she also was an addict and her man was one of the biggest drug dealers in town.

When we arrived at her place over on Steel Avenue, Cherry let us in and without my knowledge; Don pulled her aside and got some drugs from Cherry.

As I had a seat, I noticed another person in the room who caught my attention. He was very handsome. His name was Ray, who I later found out was my soon-to-be new man's best friend. We engaged in some small chit chat, which was interrupted when Don was ready to leave. I was about ready to leave, too, but intrigued by this Ray character. For some reason, Cherry invited me to stay and said she'd give me a ride home later. At that time I didn't realize she was setting me up for her man. As a matter of fact, I was still a little naïve. I was 20 years old. I did not use drugs and I was not interested in it. But from my vantage point on the outside looking in, it appeared safe and clean.

Staying around a while longer was fine with me, because I was curious about Ray and I asked Cherry questions about him. I could not get over how fine he was. I hung out so long because I wanted to be noticed by Ray.

Five hours later, West Coast Jack came through the door. If someone had told me this was going to be my new man, I wouldn't have believed them because he just wasn't my type. I like men a little taller than that. I couldn't help but notice that he couldn't take his eyes off of me. As a matter of fact, he lit up like a Christmas tree when he first saw me. My curly locks that my father so loved seemed to really captivate Jack. He kept saying, "You got good hair," and rubbing my head. The longer I sat there I began to notice how exquisitely decorated this house was. I can't begin to tell you how impressed I was. I was mesmerized by the décor. Everywhere I looked, I saw powder blue. The sofa, drapes, carpet – everything blue. I had never seen anything that beautiful. Did I say I was impressed?

Now that West Coast had my attention, he threw a huge wad of money on the floor, along with his gun, took off his shirt and sat directly across from me. Before I knew it, he had made his way over to me while talking on the phone and began caressing my knee, all the while laughing and carrying on the conversation like it was business as usual. Looking for some back up from Cherry, I was dismayed when I saw her knocked out like a light in the corner.

The heroin had gotten the best of her. West Coast Jack was a cocaine user. I believe he was in love with Cherry until she became an addict. It was somewhat of a turn-on that this man could talk to and outright hit on me right in front of his lady. It showed how powerful and out of the ordinary he was. Square men sneak out on their wives and the girlfriend they cheat with would never let them have any other woman, and a threesome suggestion could leave a man in need of first aid. But some men can totally control some women with or without drugs. He slightly kicked Cherry and told her to go to bed. She got up and told me that West Coast would take me home, but somehow I knew he had other plans for me.

Midnight rolled around quickly. I guess that was West Coast Jack's cue to focus his energy on getting me into bed with him. He invited me upstairs and for some reason I followed. The one thing

I knew for sure was Jack's next move was sex. I was persistent about not giving in to him. He put on a Curtis Mayfield tune called "Gypsy Woman," then he asked me to pour him and myself a drink. I made him some Hennessy on the rocks, but when I told him I didn't plan on drinking, I could tell it was spoiling his plans to get me to let my guard down.

That first "no" West Coast couldn't take for an answer, so he brought out the cocaine and he offered it to me. Again, I told him I didn't do that. But he was persistent, and finally my curiosity overruled my wisdom. I snorted a few lines and waited to see what would happen – if it was as amazing as everyone else had hyped it up to be. That evening was turning out to be anticlimactic. I wasn't getting any thrill, so I asked West Coast to take me home.

Before we left, West Coast posed the most off-the-wall, unintelligible question to me: "What would you do if I threw you out the window?"

I responded, "I would hold on to your butt and you would go out with me."

I had to let him know I was no push-over who he could walk all over. West Coast asked me where I lived and soon we were on our way in a red and white Fleetwood, complete with the fine, fresh smell of leather. We were rolling in style. I was relaxed because I knew I was on my way home. Not too long before my nerves started to fade, it became evident that Mr. Jack had other plans for us, as he made a turn way before he got to my side of town.

He made a stop at another of his associate's house, where he purchased some more drugs. Before went entered his friend's house, West Coast instructed me not to "get smart" with this guy, Collar. All I did was smile a nervous grin, as to not draw attention to the inner turmoil. I did not say one word. Collar asked Jack, "Where'd you get this pretty thing?" West Coast just smiled and didn't respond. He did not claim me as his woman and at that point I wasn't. West Coast made his purchase and we left. That feeling of calm returned because I assumed the next move was to my house. That did not happen. I found myself right back where I started – at his house.

Now fear was beginning to creep in. I had $300 dollars on me. It was late and I had no transportation. I reminded myself who I was dealing with – a pimp – and became even more fearful of the prospect that he might rob me. That notion isn't too far-fetched, being that West Coast already was trying to kidnap me. Once inside the house, he took me to his room, removed his shirt and commanded me to strip down. In this room was a round, red velvet bed, which was well-worn from past rendezvous with women, some who probably got acquainted with him the same way I did. I thought to myself, "Oh boy. What's next?"

But I had to let West Coast Jack know, "I'm not going to have sex with you on the first night. I don't know you."

The words that I spoke with such conviction were ineffective. He had his Hennessey and cocaine and he asked me to try some again.

I was adamant: "No, I want to go home."

I was careful not to take off my boots because I that's where I was hiding my money. I just had it in my mind that he would take all of it. The truth is he wouldn't have taken it because he had lots of money, and my measly $300 was nothing but mere pennies to West Coast Jack.

His shameless begging and my rigid rejection weren't getting me anywhere, though. We were at a stalemate. After about an hour of him harassing and trying to sweet talk me, I gave in. I figured that lying with West Coast would get me home. I felt like it was my only way out. I was interested in Jack but not to that point of intimacy. It happened so quickly. It's probably best that I remember it that way because it was void of any pleasure or emotion. Once we were finished, I knew I really had to go. I knew my mother would be upset – more than she already was – if I stayed any longer. She was watching my sons.

I asked to use the phone to call my mother, which, as I look back on the situation, I should have done in the beginning. She was extremely upset because my grandmother was seriously ill.

I could see that West Coast wasn't going to take me home. He just wanted more sex. After all of this, he told me to call a cab. I had to leave. My grandmother was dying. But that was of no consequence to West Coast, who was the epitome of selfishness. He was bold enough to ask me to make up his bed, which I refused to do. He asked if I had cab fare and, to his surprise, I said I did. If only I had the right mind to catch a cab earlier. He wasn't holding me hostage; rather, I gave up my power by submitting to his demands.

The next day at 10 a.m., I arrived tired yet comforted by the safe territory of my mom's house. After I left, I still knew very little about West Coast. I knew he had big-time paper (money). He was sweet and tender with me. I just knew I had something special in him, but as we know, things sometimes are not what they seem to be, 'cause later the real West Coast Jack would make his appearance. He was vicious and concealed his jealousy. With him, you'd never know an ass whipping was coming. He was a nice person who played it tough – a notorious woman beater, consumed with sexual desires, very smart, dangerous to women but a coward to men, and a hard-core criminal.

At 19, I had no advice from anyone on what to do with a man like West Coast. A part of me knew I should leave and never come back, but he was rich and however he made his money, it was on a very large scale. Plus, he made me feel that he couldn't get on with his life without me. So I investigated the situation. I let him choose for me and, for a while, life was beautiful. Money and expensive cars continued to impress me. It's been said that "everything comes with a price." For me, no truer words ever have been spoken. Life has its ups and downs, naturally, but bad or unwise decisions can prolong the down time.

I saw a familiar face: Poppa Swotty. He hadn't changed a bit since the last time I saw him, which was a little while ago. Sitting on the porch in his jealous rage, he threw a brick and broke my mother's window. He knew I had been out all night but he didn't have a right to act out like that, especially because we were no longer together.

It was bad enough that my mother had a strong dislike for Poppa Swotty. His cavalier disrespect only upset her more and my mom, in not so many words, told him he was going to pay for the damages. About a week later, my family and I went to the South to bury my grandma Madear. In the midst of girl talk with my sister Tulum, I began to inquire about West Coast, who she said apparently was a big drug dealer – not a pimp. The term she used was "rich nigga." It was almost like I forgot about how fearful I was and how unrelenting he was that first time we met. I was so giddy at the mention of his name that I couldn't wait to call him. I was still a kind of shy, so I asked Tulum to call for me.

As fate would have it, my period was late and I just knew I was pregnant and that West Coast Jack was the father. But suddenly, Mother Nature made her visit, which meant that I no longer had a reason to talk to West Coast. And when I did get on the phone with him, I was a little lost for words. However, being the slick talker that he was, that didn't matter as much. West Coast asked me how was I doing and expressed his sympathy for my loss, and, in the same breath, invited me over to his place.

"So, what are you doing right now?" I asked him.

"Oh, just ummm lying in bed," West Coast said. I thought this was slightly weird because it was only 4 p.m. – way too early for bed. "Why don't you join me?"

"Who you got in that bed with you?" I asked in a half-serious, half-joking manner.

"Don't worry about who's in the bed with me. You just come over and get in with me."

That was a huge turn-off to me. I let him know that he wouldn't be seeing me that night. In reality, I waited a few months before that happened. I still felt slightly insecure about this West Coast Jack but came to the conclusion that I did like him and that we needed to connect. So I decided to go over to his house.

I went out of town to Chicago and when I came back, I got with West Coast Jack. Further turmoil ensued when I needed to move my furniture out of Poppa Swotty's house. He wanted to keep my stuff. Not surprisingly, he had a fit and tried to stop me, the sorry son of a bitch. He said I wasn't going to get anything. That's when I called the police and when they came, he told them that I couldn't have the furniture – which was mine – unless I gave him $500. At this point, it wasn't worth the stress or wasted energy trying to reason with Poppa Swotty, so I told him he could have the money, but he'd have to come over and get it because I didn't have $500 on me. But in my mind, I knew he wasn't getting one red cent out of me. Sure enough, the next day Poppa was knocking at my door.

I answered with a major attitude: "Nigga, did you really think that I was going to give you $500? Fuck you. I'm not with you no more. I'm with West Coast Jack."

Poppa Swotty was so furious that he left out the door and I didn't see him for a while. About six months later, he found out my address at the new house I moved into. We got into it and he had the audacity to pour beer into our baby son Little Man's eyes after he told him that West Coast was his daddy. It really was over between us.

West Coast Jack would prove to be the undoing of me. The things I suffer from today, and perhaps the rest of my life, started with him.

CHAPTER 4:

Life in the Fast Lane

Going downhill in a vehicle with no brakes or steering wheel, traveling at speeds that are too fast to get off.

N ow that West Coast Jack and I had gotten together, for the first time in my life I was beginning to experience what love really was, and it couldn't have come at a better time: Christmas of 1971.

West Coast was far different from Poppa Swotty, who never would have lifted a finger to make my wants and desires of having a special Christmas a reality. I fixed my little white house up for the holidays and West Coast Jack's house was also decked out, complete with twinkling lights, garland and a nice, tall Christmas tree. It was like something out of a magazine. The joy of the season was in abundance and I had peace of mind.

I was hanging out at West Coast's house on Christmas Eve and was about to go home to get my boys' Christmas together -- you know, placing the gifts under the tree and completing the finishing touches. But knowing my luck with assembling things, I told West Coast that I needed a man to help put my son's Big Wheel together, as well as some other toys. Although he couldn't come, he sent his little brother, Billy, home with me to do the job; West Coast promised me he'd be over on Christmas Day to spend time with my little ones and me. That was fine with me.

I was just happy because I knew and felt that this man really loved me. West Coast Jack always was so nice to my boys. It was almost like we were one happy family, as we were in the midst of our at honeymoon phase. He treated me like I was his precious little angel at that time.

Unlike Jack, Billy stood about 6 feet, 5 inches tall. His stature was intimidating, but he always treated me with respect, so I had no reason to fear him. At about 4 a.m. on Christmas Eve, Billy left my house to head back to West Coast's house. Now something serious was getting ready to jump off with these really big dope men. No one was prepared for what was about to unfold.

As Billy entered Jack's home, he saw his brother writhing on the floor in a puddle of blood and four guys high-tailing it out of the house. Without hesitating, he ran toward Jack and picked up his gun to shoot the intruders, but Jack, who we soon would find out had been shot twice in the leg, pleaded with Billy to not shot.

The vicious intruders just happened to be West Coast Jack's friends, Frank and Lefty, and their two henchmen. Frank and Lefty were partners who had a reputation around the way for acting recklessly, never thinking twice about the dirt they were doing. Lefty, the more crazy of the two, was so heartless that he also broke a whiskey bottle and jammed it into West Coast's face, right under his eye. There were certain things that you just weren't supposed to mess with, another man's woman being the main thing.

"So what's this shit I hear 'bout you and my bitch shacking up?" Lefty spat at West Coast, demanding answers.

"What, nigga? She told me you wudn't handlin' yoe bidness, so I gave her a taste of what a real nigga could do for her," West Coast Jack snapped back. "And boy, do I do it well."

"Oh, is that so? Well, who's the real nigga now?" Lefty said, reaching into is jacket and pulling out his heat.

Before Jack could come back with some cutting comeback, he was staring down the barrel of a pistol. Lefty had that wild look in his eye, as if to say, "Say sumthin' else, nigga," but instead of shooting West Coast in that bucket head of his, he fired two quick shots below the waist. West Coast tested the water and got burnt. He paid the price with two bullets that pierced through his right leg, right down to the bone. Now, just how West Coast Jack ended up in that predicament was a long time coming. This all went down because of his other vice: sex.

Janice, a tall, dark-skinned girl from New York, had been staying at her man, Lefty's, home, as she had a special role transferring dope for these big shots. But she really wanted West Coast Jack, so much so that they were messing around. Girls chose guys who were big time, because they figured that those types of fast-life guys can do more for them. The name of the game was cop and blow. The pimps were so slick and conniving that they would steal another man's woman right from under his arm, and would jump at the chance to spit game to women who already were spoken for, and if so, that was too bad for you.

I wish that carefree feeling of being in love with Jack would have lasted longer. Not soon after falling head over heels for him, I realized he was demanding and controlling with a volatile temper. He had no morals. He would have your mother, sister, daughter or niece. It really didn't matter who it was. Still, despite his wrongdoings, I stood by his side. I guess you can say I was blinded by love, even though he was brazen in his disrespect for me, the woman who he had talked about creating a future with.

West Coast was rushed to the Detroit Receiving Hospital, where he stayed for 30 days. It seemed so out of character for him to break his promise to spend the holiday with me, so I just knew something was up. Billy broke the news to me at about 4 p.m. on Christmas Day over the phone, and I rushed over to the hospital. As he was recovering and all of his family members were there to visit him, about 30 or so women also were there, both old and new girlfriends. I was no fool; I knew there were other women, but not to this extent. They were all coming at all different times, so I saw them but I didn't care because I knew he really cared about me. These women were used to sharing their man. To them, I was just another link in the chain. Instead of leaving West Coast while he was in bad shape, I stayed. I stood back, watching all of them, not knowing any of them except Cherry. She was one of his first women when he became a big dope man, but just like that, West Coast fell out of love with Cherry because got hooked on that heroin, blowing it up her nose.

Mind you, this very, very big dope man West Coast didn't have any medical insurance. At one point during the ordeal, West Coast needed 30 pints of blood. I'd do anything for my man, so I went with the nurse and gave him a pint of blood. When visiting hours ended, me and Cherry went back to my house to wind down, just sitting around talking about everything. Cherry was real cool and open with me, like we were old friends. She put me up on a lot about West Coast Jack, letting me in on the sleazy details about him and her and his other women. I didn't care about his other women, as long as they didn't say anything to me -- and at that time they didn't.

West Coast wanted me down at the hospital to visit him every day and I there I was, right there at his bedside. He had a cast on his left leg from the thigh to the ankle. Being stuck in that hospital bed and suffering those painful bullet wounds didn't stifle West Coast's sex drive. Oh, no! He wanted me to have sex with him while he still was in the hospital ward. We gave it a try, but I didn't feel comfortable doing that. The women, the 30 within 30 days, they slowly but surely stopped coming around to see him, but I was there every single day for that month.

Now one of his women, Rosie, was about 17 years old and had a daughter with Jack. She came to the hospital to visit him as she was about seven or eight months pregnant with his son, who she named Abdul. West Coast also had a son named Earl by Rosie's cousin. Now, West Coast was a man who went through his women's families. For the time being, I thought I was the exception to his pattern. I don't think he loved Rosie; in fact, I didn't feel threatened by her at all. She wasn't attractive. She had a lot of bumps on her face. Rosie had long hair, but because she was young, West Coast had a thing for her. He had things for a number of different women, and with the women came the babies. When I first met him, he already had at least 10 kids – that I knew of – by I can't tell you how many different women. West Coast had four by a girl named Dianne, a Muslim who was his high school sweetheart. There was the two he had with Rosie, one by Slick, and an older son by Candy, who lives in New York. There was a son called Clever. There was at least one other little girl by some woman whose name I don't know. He had all these kids -- practically as much as a baseball team -- by the time he was 21 years old!

West Coast knew he did not take care of all of these children. He would give Dianne money sometimes, but that task involved a little espionage and detective work. She had to track him down, pop over to his house and sit and wait, and then he'd give her a little change for her four kids. Although I had such strong feelings for him, West Coast and I never had children together. I did become pregnant twice by him but lost the babies, one that I had aborted.

His mother Emma loved her son so much. She thought he was the richest kingpin of all. Ms. Emma was very close with all of his women, even me. They told her a lot about their relationships with West Coast and always gave her gifts, myself included. When West Coast Jack was discharged from the hospital, I went to pick him up. At the time, he had a white Fleetwood Cadillac but the police had it in impounded because of some dope deal that went down. Long story short, he got it back. But after 30 days of being bed-ridden in the hospital, West Coast had gotten broke. He still had his house on Outer Drive and the fancy ride, but no money. I brought him some clothes down there to wear home. Being at the house was almost worse than him being confined to that hospital bed. He had to stay inside on crutches for at least a month. Couldn't do anything for him. That's when he wanted me to live with him at his place and take care of him, and I did. So I let my brother JB and his wife and kids move into my house on Steel. Betty, JB's wife, took care of my two sons while I was taking care of West Coast at his house.

Back at West Coast's house, the women still came in and out. This one girl in particular, named Chickie, stuck out in my mind. Her man was a real crazy pimp, East Side. She ended up leaving East Side and stayed for about a week on Outer Drive, liking West Coast. Cherry, she was there on and off because she stayed over at a friend's house because West Coast was not too much interested in her any more. He really liked me. I was very shy and quiet, and I didn't talk too much. I am so happy to be with a man who isn't fighting me. We were three solid months into the relationship and West Coast hadn't put his hands on me. It was a good feeling. But the other women were starting to wear on me and came to a head one night as West Coast and I were laying in his plush, all-gold king size bed in his master bedroom. I was so upset when I began to think about him fooling around with other women, but I was tired of keeping my emotions bottled up inside.

So I said to him, "You know you better not ever make me sleep with you or none of your other women."

Hoping to get the assurance that he wouldn't demand such a deplorable thing of me, I was completely disillusioned when he didn't utter a single word.

About a year later, West Coast Jack and I still were going strong. He still hadn't ever hit me. Out of the blue he said, "Baby Girl, you remember when you told me to not ever make me go to bed with you and my other females?"

I replied, "Yes, I remember."

"I haven't, have I?"

He was right. "No, you haven't," I responded.

But that didn't mean that West Coast had left all those other women alone. He and Cherry broke up, but West Coast didn't want her to be with another man. Cherry was a nice-looking, light-skinned girl, but she wore thick glasses because she had the eyesight of a bat. One night when West Coast saw Cherry in the after-hours joint, she got smart with him when he called her. It didn't take much to set West Coast off, 'cause the next thing she knew, he shattered a glass and carved a long cut on her face, down by the side of her ear. That incident really signaled the end of those two.

Still, there was Sheila, the Playboy bunny who was cute, thanks in part to the extra-long fake hair she wore. She was petite and fixed herself up nicely, but she was so fake. Nonetheless, West Coast truly loved Sheila, but she was just about done with him when I came into the picture. He beat her up so badly that she had to have a plate surgically implanted into her head. He hurt her plenty of times. West Coast was jealous because all the player-type men wanted her. Sheila would go and lay up with some of his friends, like Lefty and Frank, and they paid her for sex.

West Coast Jack, still broke, didn't have big-time money anymore, so he made connections to get back on his feet and get him back in that balla status again. And he did, at which point Sheila decided to get back with him for about six months. I was heartbroken that he would even entertain the idea of bringing that tramp around, knowing what she's done. That was the final straw. In a fit of rage, I packed up all my clothes and stormed out of his house – with the door wide open. I moved back to my mother's house on Mackey. About three days later, West Coast came over to my mother's house to talk to me. I thought, "What took you so long?" And here was trying to win me back.

"You know I love you, girl," West Coast said to me in that sweet tone. "I'm getting ready to go to the top, like I used to be. You want to go with me?"

"You know I do."

"Alright now, but you can't be up and leaving me like that."

And that was all it took for us to rekindle our relationship. I proceeded with caution though, and continued to live with my mom.

West Coast soon met this very big, square, nerd-looking guy named DC He was really big in the dope game. His whole family -- at least 10 brothers -- all had huge, expensive houses and cars. DC became West Coast Jack's partner, and Jack got back on his feet and started making big-time money again. One day in late winter, he came over to my mother's house to get me. West Coast wanted me to go to New York to take $60,000, buy a kilo of heroin there and smuggle it back on the airplane to Detroit. Being that I was no millionaire, that seemed like good money for such a small task. Of course I was in; I would do anything West Coast said. So I met DC at his house to count the money. It was all in the name of love that I was going along with this drug deal, but as DC and West Coast handed over the $60,000 to me in a briefcase and dropped me off at the airport, I grew nervous. I had never done anything like this before.

Thankfully, I landed safely in New York, which was the very large city that I envisioned it to be. I had reservations at this upscale hotel and when the cab pulled up, the bell hop opened up the taxi door, snatched the briefcase and ran into the hotel with it. The hotel was having some sort of convention, which meant there were a whole lot of people inside. The bell hop was running among this sea of people. "Was that supposed to happen? Where is he going with the loot? Will I make it out of the Big Apple unscathed?" These were among the many thoughts that crossed my mind as my heart raced a mile a minute.

I dashed out of the cab without paying the fare, and chased after the bell hop, running into all kinds of people and not knowing where the front desk was located. I absolutely had to keep my eye on that bell hop. Well, he took the briefcase filled with the $60,000 and casually set it on the floor right by the front desk. At this point, I realized that he just was doing his job by handling my bag. Still panicked, I picked up the briefcase and looked around to see that the driver had chased me, demanding that I pay up for the cab fare I ducked out on. He was hollering and carrying on, and drawing attention when he really didn't need to. I reached into my pocket and handed him some money. "Whew, that was a close call." Finally, I checked in with the desk clerk, paid for my room and I went up to the 20th floor, with the room key in hand. A white man in a business suit followed me all the way to my floor, and when we were the only two hotel guests left on the elevator, he nonchalantly asked me, "How much do you charge?"

I still was fuming about what had just happened with the bell hop and the cab driver that I just snapped back at him, "How much do *you* charge?"

That white man looked so surprised, but it sure did shut him up. I got off the elevator and proceeded to my room. This big guy named Ron had flown into New York with me to make the connections, but he didn't sit with me on the plane. He came to my room and he retrieved the briefcase, which he understood I was supposed to give to him for the deal. I stayed in the city for about three days and made the most of my time there by going shopping, spending the $1,000 that I was paid to make this run. The first day, I spent about $600 on some clothes and came back with about $400. When I returned from that jaunt, Ron brought white heroin to my room and told me to go buy myself a girdle – this would be the disguise for me to transport the drugs back on the airplane. So I did as I was told and returned to my hotel room. A rookie to the sport of smuggling, I wasn't quite sure how the professionals do this thing with the dope in the girdle and still are able to walk. Cautious so that I looked normal, I took the heroin – it amounted to a kilo of drugs – and put it in my bag in a wrap made of hotel towels. Ron, who was hooked on heroin, had punched holes in the dope bag, took some of the drugs out and blew it up his nose. The two of us made it to the airport, all the while acting like we were perfect strangers. I had my doubts about if our cover would be blown. I didn't even want to ponder the "what ifs," but both my mind and heart were racing. I had to be cool, though. I held my breath as I sent the bag through the checkpoint. After what felt like an hour had passed, I rejoiced on the inside when the bag went through without any problems. And when I made it onto that airplane, I told myself that I'd never do anything crazy like that again. Everything arrived back to Detroit just fine, and upon my arrival, I gave West Coast Jack the dope. He and DC are both happy that I had it.

Now DC and West Coast had set up shop at this house on the west side of Detroit on Compass Street. My sister's boyfriend, Lewis, spent so many hours there every day, running the house and selling their drugs. That place was fixed up so that if the police came to bust them, they couldn't get in -- no matter how hard they tried. I mean, it was on some secret agent, spy shit. This was all of DC's doing. There was even a trap door on the front porch that acted as an elevator that would drop down to the basement. That house was off the chain.

A month later, West Coast and DC were ready for me to take another dope trip, now to California. It was the same deal. They paid me $1,000 and I took another $60,000 over there. This time the heroin was a dark, dark brown. It reminded me of that thick Algae syrup. I boarded the plane go to California all by myself this time, but I was excited to see this new place in person and see if it was like it was on the TV shows and in the movies. When I touched down at LAX, a guy named JJ picked me up. Right off the bat, he liked me. I kind of liked him, too. JJ was an older, tall and handsome man, who was pushing a clean Cadillac El Dorado. I was looking forward to what the next three days would have in store for us, what kind of trouble we could get into. When I got into JJ's car, I gave him the money and we went partying with it. We went to some dance clubs, including this joint called "Name of the Game." I was about 22 or 23 years old and I liked to dance, so JJ and I went to about three nightclubs that evening. We tore the dance floor up, partied and had fun. West Coast Jack didn't cross my mind once. Afterward, JJ took me to a hotel, where I stayed for the duration of the trip to Los Angeles. He left to go home -- I guess to his wife – but came back for me the next day. We rode around all day long while he took care of his business. JJ treated me really nice, took me to breakfast, lunch, and dinner and really showed me a good time, being that this was my first time in California. A girl could get used to this summertime weather in the middle of February. I loved Detroit though. The last day I was in L.A., I went back to JJ's apartment and he wanted to have sex with me. I mean, he was attractive and all, but I didn't want to. And I don't know why, but I did. All it was that night was plain old sex. The next day was time for me to fly back to Detroit from LAX. I had some time to kill before my flight, so JJ took me to some bar where there was nothing but Mexican men who didn't speak any English. JJ wanted me to stay at this bar all day until he came back with the drugs, so I did. I didn't know where the bar was but I did notice that there weren't too many buildings around. Not fond of alcohol, I just wasted away at that seedy bar, waiting on JJ to come back for me. Throughout this timeframe, 10 or 15 Mexican men and offer me $5 to have sex with them. I was so mad and I was getting very upset with them. I thought they were crazy asking me that. So many of them took turns coming back and forth asking me the same thing. They could tell I wasn't from around there. At about 8 that night, a black guy -- JJ's friend who had come to check on me. JJ had coached me to say that I was his woman to anybody who asked me who I was, so I did. This black guy came in and got a beer, sat and talked with me until JJ came back, and I was happy about that because I had some decent company to talk to. When I mentioned to him that I was JJ's lady, he said, "How do you like your man JJ being a cop?"

When he said that, my head almost fell off of my body. So, I thought within a flash, "I gotta play this one off … Cop? What the hell have I gotten myself into?" I made up some crap about me finding a man in a uniform irresistible and told him how happy I was that we were together. I was believable, but I needed to get up out of there before the friend started asking me more questions and forcing me to formulate a web of lies. It was too much to handle. I tried not to raise any alarm as I left the bar to "go to the restaurant across the street and get me something to eat." In actuality, I went to the phone booth across the way and called West Coast back in Detroit. I was terrified since learning that JJ was an officer of the law, and I just had to fill him in on this shocking development. West Coast immediately gave the phone over to DC.

"What the hell is going on, DC? You got me over here hangin' with a cop. This shit is starting to get out of control," I screamed into the receiver. I wanted answers, and I wanted them ASAP, damn it.

"Calm the fuck down! Calm down. I don't know where you're getting that from, but JJ ain't no damn policeman," DC replied, in an attempt to allay my doubts. "What I look like sendin' you out there to meet up with some cop?"

But hearing that wasn't enough to stop me from going into panic mode. At that point, I didn't know whose word to take or who I could trust. That really messed with my mind. DC still was rambling on, but I wasn't hearing anything he was saying. The next voice I heard on the other end was West Coast.

"Baby Girl, you straight. For real. Don't worry 'bout nothing,'" he said.

"Look, I ain't touchin' that dope. If you want it back with you in Detroit, you betta find some way to pick this shit up from the airport," I retorted.

"Aight … Aight. I'ma be there," West Coast assured me.

In the meantime, I had to play it off, despite my insurmountable fears taking over.

JJ soon returned with the heroin and he called DC and West Coast to inform them that he took care of business and was ready to put me on the airplane. I kept telling myself, "Be cool, Baby Girl. This will all be over soon." JJ drove me to LAX, but when we got to the drop-off curb, he acted like he didn't want to help me with my bags. So I asked him, "You aren't going to take my bags into the airport?" I was thinking quickly on my toes, remembering that I told West Coast I wasn't touching anything. JJ complied, hugged me and left. The anxiety was so bad that my heart felt like it was going to beat out of my chest. I called DC back, hoping he could say something to make me less scared.

"Baby Girl, I did some checking on JJ, and he is a security guard -- but like a police security guard -- and he does carry a gun," DC reported.

"Listen, I don't care. You or West Coast's ass better be at that airport in the morning to get this bag because I ain't touching it."

"OK, OK. We'll be there."

Well, that fleeting peace of mind was nowhere to be found, when contrary to what was planned, West Coast Jack and DC both were no-shows at the Detroit Metro Airport. Surprise, surprise.

I walked downstairs to get my bag, and I was the very last person to pick up luggage from the baggage claim. I kept looking around to see if I see any policemen were standing nearby. Seeing none, I snatched the bag and ran outside, jumped into a cab and went straight to West Coast's house. This Negro had the nerve to open the door with a grin on his face. Man, was I pissed, but then I calmed down because I didn't have to worry anymore. I made it safely home. I went my mother's house, where my kids were.

Mom hadn't asked me why I was gone. She didn't know where I went but just like a mother, she figured something I was doing wasn't right. I still had the $1,000 they paid me because I hadn't shopped in California, so I gave it to my mother and my baby sister, Sugar. They were both fine with that. They always kept my kids because I would pay them well, making them offers they couldn't refuse. Still blindly in love with West Coast, I wanted to move back into his house, but he and Sheila had gotten back together. West Coast had money and then was deeply in love with Sheila -- they were dressing alike and doing things together. I was very hurt by their romance, but I felt trapped because I wanted to get out of my mother's house. West Coast came to my rescue and told me to go find a house for sale and that he'd buy it for me. That made me oh so happy, so I went and talked with a Realtor and he found me a nice, small, two-bedroom house for me on the west side of Detroit on Mark Twain Avenue. It was perfect for me and my two sons Carlos and Little Man. I got the house promptly and moved us in. If you thought I was head over heels for West Coast Jack back then, now I was over the moon enamored with this man for buying me a house to call my own. To add icing to this cake of good tidings, West Coast and DC gave me a car. It was a Monte Carlo that had been one of DC's old cars, but it was nice to have transportation for the first time in a long time.

My earlier mistakes are now being compounded with my continuance in this lifestyle. What seemed like a step up in life (I was making good money) was, in reality, going down with a steady pull. Check yourself. You could be headed north when you think you're headed south.

CHAPTER 5:

Baby Girl's Indoctrination to Boosting School

From the skillet to the frying pan, we find Baby Girl waist deep and sinking in the quicksand of the fast life.

One of the patterns I've noticed with my life is how quickly things can go from sugar to shit. I really felt that things were looking up for me and West Coast. But after a mere three months in that cute, little house that he bought me, West Coast Jack was sent off to prison.

Little did I know, this wasn't his first time in the pen. He actually was busted a few times before I met him, messing around with that stuff.

One time his stupid behind was going to the airport to pick up somebody who was bringing a kilo of heroin from New York to Detroit. All of West Coast's real big connections came out of New York. After he got his associate, they headed down Interstate 94 East back to West Coast's house, but as luck would have it, he ran out of gas in his red and white Fleetwood. Jack ran up the freeway ramp to get some gas and when he came back, the Feds were there. They busted him and his heroin-toting friends, sent them off to jail, confiscated the stash of drugs and impounded his car. West Coast had a big dope case on his hands, and he hired one of the best attorneys in Detroit who got him off scot-free. He even got his car back.

West Coast got off easy that time, but after a few run-ins with the law, the judge wanted to teach him a lesson by giving him a sentence of 7 to 15 years behind bars. I was oblivious to the fact that West Coast had any of these cases pending.

West Coast never let me go to court with him, so before he went to prison one day I came over to his house, only to find a notice nailed to the tree in his front yard. A foreclosure was taking place and he was losing the house. I removed the paper and gave it to him, but he could care less. I guess he acted that way because he knew he was getting locked up. And then it just happened. West Coast Jack went to court and didn't come back home.

I was so in love with him at the time, so knowing that he wouldn't be free for several years messed me up mentally and emotionally. I didn't want to talk to anyone, not even my family. I felt so done.

When he went to prison, Sheila dropped him like a hot potato. I became the one taking charge of his house on Outer Drive. I was moving the furniture, and his mother and all of his sisters took everything. Damn leeches. I got the baby grand piano that no one wanted and the family room furniture and one of the king-sized bedroom sets. The rest of his family all came in and took, took, took. It was almost as if their sadness about West Coast was pushed aside when it came to getting his fancy belongings.

His mother came up nicely, taking a gold bedroom set that about 100 of his women had slept in. His mom was really crazy about him, and she knew all of his business, partly because West Coast would tell her all kinds of stuff. Oddly enough, she loved hearing all about what was going on between him and his women.

Fortunately, he never brought those broads around me. They knew me but I didn't know them, unless they called the house looking for Mr. West Coast. This one floozy called herself getting smart with me. She would soon find out that she was fuckin' with the wrong girl.

I answered the phone and heard a female voice on the other end of the receiver saying, "Let me talk to West Coast."

"He's sleep."

"Then wake him up."

"Naw, bitch. You come wake his ass up." I was starting to get mad.

"Aight then. I will."

Click.

Oh, was I heated! I went into my closet and got my .38-caliber handgun and was waiting outside for that bitch to roll through. About 10 minutes later, here she comes, pulling up into the driveway. But when she had seen that I had brought some help along the way, she sped off. It was a small victory, but battling off the women was a constant struggle. I accepted it though, because that's how it had been from Jump Street. West Coast Jack always had a group of women chasing after him. I didn't have to be in their mix. I let him know, "I ain't cut like that, brotha." His womanizing was the main reason why my mother despised him. She pretended to get along with him for my sake, but I knew that they would never see eye to eye.

My mom ended up having a seizure behind his nonsense. One day, West Coast stormed into the bedroom and locked the door behind him. I knew that meant he was in there sniffing drugs. A short while later, he came out. Instinctively, my mother opened the top dresser drawer and found his stash of coke and all the supplies that accompanied it. She hit the floor, and began having another episode.

I remember one time he went to county jail for a few days and the bail bondsman that he knew very well. Goldstar in the 1970s and '80s was the biggest bonding company in Detroit. West Coast needed someone to put up a house for him. In his more abundant days, he had all of that money he didn't buy his mother a house, and years later when his mother died he didn't attend her funeral. He returned back to jail on some dope-related charges.

My ex-husband, Poppa Swotty, and I had bought a house together on Archdale in Detroit. I no longer was with him but I still had the deed to that house, which was worth something. I got a guy to pretend he was Poppa Swotty and we took the deed to Goldstar Bonding to bail out West Coast using me and Poppa Swotty's house. West Coast Jack then was a free man, thanks to my thinking. I did for him what none of his other women would even think to do. I know that he had five or six main women who owned homes renting out their properties to rack up enough money to get him out of jail.

At this point, I had spent every penny I had trying to get West Coast released from being locked up. But West Coast's drug habit was calling -- he wanted some cocaine. And the nerve of his mother, giving me $50 and told me to give it to him so he could buy some cocaine. What kind of mother gives her grown child an allowance to satisfy his addiction?

After catching a few big cases, West Coast was sentenced to 7 □ to 15 years, but he only served three years in federal prison in Oakland. Something major was about to go down, as West Coast was detained in Cook County Jail in Michigan, about 30 miles from Detroit. As they say, absence makes the heart grow fonder and I was excited to pay my man a visit. I was living on Mark Twain in the house that he bought me and being there without him only made me miss him more. I was looking forward to seeing him, but West Coast asked me to smuggle in some weed by putting it into a magazine book, folding a page and sticking it in there. I loved West Coast and would do almost anything for him, but I wasn't down with doing some mess that could get me caught up, too. So had my girlfriend take the book up to the counter at the jail and leave it. When the officer went through the book, he found the marijuana but she left out without a trace because I put the magazine in another guy's name. That was an unsuccessful plot, but it was OK because from the inside, West Coast Jack used his slick mouth to become friendly with one of the guards, who let him break out of jail for five or six hours. We had it set up so that I would give the guard some heroin to pass along to West Coast. Every time a transaction was made, I had would have to give the police $200. I did this about seven or eight times.

One of the inmates overdosed in the utility closet and the federal police came in to investigate. But before they interrogated the police officer, Mike, who was working with West Coast, he let him and some others go out to a hotel, dropped them off and told them to be back at 4 that morning. I picked West Coast Jack up from the hotel in his prison suit, but he changed clothes into a sharp outfit and we drove back to Detroit. First, he went to see his friend, Slim, who is another big dope man. I don't know how much cocaine he gave him, but Slim supplied Jack with enough to take back with him. It was a whirlwind trip, as we were pressed for time. While he was out, he wanted to get what he was being deprived of behind those prison walls. West Coast wanted me to take him to Sheila's house and I did. I waited in the car while he went in and had sex with her. From there, we headed back to my house on Mark Twain. We made the most of what little time we had together. I helped West Coast take down his hair weave and later, we had sex.

But the time quickly came for me to take West Coast back to the hotel, where Mike would take him back to the county jail. On our way back, we got stopped by the sheriff because I was driving so fast in a rush to get him back. The officer asked me if I knew how fast I was driving. Through a pounding chest and tense lips, I managed to slip out, "No, sir." The officer then asked West Coast his name. I told him to say he is my brother JB, and I guess the policeman bought it because he let us go. By the time we made it back to the hotel it was 5 a.m. -- an hour after the planned meet-up time -- and Mike and the others had left and gone back to the Cook County Jail. I can't even begin to describe the fear that set in. What the hell were we going to do now? But being a man of his word, West Coast told me to drive him all the way back to the jail because he had promised Mike that he would be at the designated place at the set time. We arrived at the jail, but how West Coast would get back behind those walls without his cover being blown was beyond me. Thinking quickly, West Coast told me to go in and try to pretend like I was bonding some guy out. The clerk said the fictional person I was hoping to see released was not eligible for release because he was in for murder chargers. The plan was working, because as I came out, Mike saw me on the monitor and made the monitors go static, giving him the chance to open the garage and allow West Coast to run in. I went back home and the jail know anything about our little adventure.

That was, of course, until the guards noticed West Coast's drastic change in appearance, going from a weave to a short haircut. Security already was heightened with all the previous mess of the inmate overdosing, so the Feds conducted an investigation and caught wind of Mike's role. He was put in jail. Mike got out on bond and contacted. We ended up meeting and Mike told me everything that happened: He was going to serve six months in jail. Mike said he wasn't going to bring me down with him -- which he could have easily done -- because I always was so honest and straight with him. I did not have to worry; he just wanted to let me know. West Coast got shipped out to Oakland prison right away and we never heard anything about that any more.

Now West Coast is in Oakland still wanting me to bring dope into the prison, which I did. The way he got it was through the trustees in the prison. They had me to put it in the stash in a trash can, and when they cleaned up the visitor's room they would get the dope I had dropped off and took it back into the prison to give to West Coast. I would go back to visit West Coast the next day and see a fresh needle mark on his arm. When I asked him to explain himself, he tried to downplay it and say that he had shot some cocaine. I believe he was shooting heroin. Now, sometimes I would get high with him. You know, snort a few lines of coke, but that was only once in a while. That's something I could never get fully immersed in -- nor did I desire to -- being that I had two little boys. I would make the six-hour-long drive down to Oakland every other week, and then every other weekend for two years. I would go into the prison to have sex with West Coast. We would sneak off to our secret spot: the women's bathroom.

A few times I took his mother to visit him and I paid all of the expenses. One time, his mom and I were visiting with West Coast and he had the nerve to tell her that he wanted me to give him some. I wish he wasn't so bold about making his lustful desires known -- at least not in front of his mother, of all people. Even more startling was that his mother in return said to me, "My baby boy wants you to have sex with him, so you gone 'head and give some." I said to myself that she ain't right.

West Coast's baby momma, Shay, also would come to visit him. He went into the bathroom with her to have sex and they got caught. As a result, the prison terminated her visits. Just before that happened, I went down there with a girl on the weekend to pick up her man who was getting released. I didn't let West Coast know I was coming and who walks into the prison visiting area to see him? None other than Shay.

He was flamboyant, flashy and loved coochie -- basically a nympho. No matter how he got it, he was happy as long as he was getting it. He went down on women. That's what got women hooked. He knew what he was doing. Shay and I were in the visiting room waiting for West Coast to come out. She was sitting on one side and I was on the other. This is not my idea of a good surprise. West Coast didn't even flinch when he saw the two of us.

"Come on," he said. "Let's all sit together."

"Fuck you, nigga! I ain't sitting with yoe ass or that bitch. Who tha fuck you think I am?"

And just like that, I stormed out and rode 600 miles back home to Detroit.

If I had thought about my worth and how I deserve much better for myself after that eye-opening situation, I probably would have found true happiness a bit sooner. But I was used to West Coast. I'm sad to say that I missed him dearly, so that memory got pushed to the back of my mind. It wasn't long before I had gotten over it, moved down there and got the job at CBS. I moved my baby son, Lil' Man, with me, while my mother kept the oldest boy, Carlos. Now me and my son are now living in Oakland. Lil' Man, then about 6 or 7 years old, was in school. Things started looking up for us. West Coast was moved from out of the prison over to the honor camp. This new location allowed him to come out every day, Monday through Friday. He even was going to Oakland College. My apartment was in the downtown area of the city, so our sexual escapades become a daily occurrence. But before I could get comfortable with the idea of him being in my company, he was off on the next bus back up to the prison. That is something he never did before until he got into prison. Every day West Coast Jack came over, wanting to have anal sex. Wanting to please my man, I tried it a few times, but I stopped him when I started bleeding out of my rear. It was kind of selfish of him to demand the activity, in which only he gained satisfaction.

West Coast soon went home on a furlough and left me down there, which aggravated me because I moved to Indiana specifically to be closer to him. You would think that on his extended time out, he would want to spend it with me. His mother had become sick, and while he was at home with her, he caught a disease called trichomoniasis and came back and gave it to me. Within a couple of months, West Coast would be released from prison because his attorney, Lewis, had gone back to court and had West Coast brought back to Detroit. His attorney got his time cut from 7 ½ to 15 years, so that he did 3 years and was released.

While I was down there working at CBS I bought my first car, a Trans-Am. It was gray and black with an eagle on the hood. But after being in Indiana for a while, I felt it was time to go back home to Detroit. I quit my job, picked up West Coast from prison and we both drive back with my son Lil' Man. Little did I know that my excitement about West Coast's return with me would be ruined by Shay; who was throwing him a "coming home" party, which I was not invited to. Further adding to my anger was the fact that West Coast Jack went right back into the dope game, as if he didn't just get through serving a three-year sentence behind bars.

When he left to go to prison, he was hooked up with D.C., a major dealer, but when he got out in the summer of 1973, his connection was nowhere to be found. West Coast immediately got hooked up with some other dope dealers like Slim and he was back to selling heroin, which fueled his love of blowing cocaine up his nose. I was staying upstairs at his mother's house and I hated every minute of it; meanwhile, Jack is staying with his women Nickie,

Shay, Mary and all the rest at their nice houses. He was such a user and a manipulator.

West Coast's mother would tell me about all of his women sleeping together. It was a crazy situation, but I especially couldn't stand Shay. She just was plain ugly and she went with a dyke named Dee Dee, who sold West Coast's brother, Billy, some bad cocaine. Billy and Shay's brother Lynn were mad and demanded their money back, but that dyke wasn't budging. Billy ended up stabbing her in the neck, trying to kill her. He actually left her for dead, but Dee Dee pulled the knife out of her neck and called the police. For that nonsense Lynn and Billy both ended up sentenced to 10 years in prison. Shay was still going with West Coast, and of course he couldn't stand Dee Dee for messing around with his baby's momma.

West Coast had another brother named Luster, who had been in prison for about 15 years. He boxed on the same card with Tom Hicks, which meant that they both spar on the same night against different people. Luster was good and ready for his first three fights. He won but after that he started letting his heroin use take over his life. He slowly began to fade away from the boxing scene after several losses. About a year later Luster was killed.

I just wasn't happy with living with West Coast's mother. It was a nightmare. I mean his mom really liked me. The issue was that they had mice that would dart from corner to corner and shoot under the couch. It was like they had taken over. West Coast's mom acted as if they weren't running wild throughout her house. My major fear of rodents developed in childhood. One morning when my dad went to wake me up to get ready for school, there was a mouse sitting on my chest. My father screamed to alert me, and I jumped out of bed with my skin crawling. Eek! Ever since then I've been terrified of those sneaky, disease-carrying varmints. I eventually left and started living with my sister, Sugar.

I figured that I needed to make some extra cash, so I got back into contact with my friend, Rita, who has one of the best boosters in Detroit. Rita's man was Ray, the guy who I met the same night I met West Coast Jack at his house. She taught me all the techniques. I would go out to the major department stores and snatch up the most expensive clothes, placing items in my girdle. Another fail-proof trick was using a screwdriver to cut off the sensors. Rita taught me how to steal mink coats and ultra-suede. She taught me well. I was a quick study. It was a yearlong, intensive training that meant guaranteed success. At first, I watched and blocked for Rita and she would give me two $300 outfits in return. Seeing how easy it was, I got to thinking that I could boost with the best of them. Rita got a little jealous though, when I started doing it on my own, but she saw how good I was and decided, if you can't beat 'em, join 'em.

We didn't steal anything that cost less than $100. My boosting dress alone was $600. We would go from city to city and state to state boosting. We would drive all over Houston, Memphis, Alabama, St. Louis, Miami and scores of other towns. We would just pick a state from the road map, book a flight and rent a car to get us from boutique to department store to any place with expensive brands.

Sugar, my younger sister, would always take care of my kids and I paid her $100 to $300 for watching them during my jaunts. A lot of the time, she would keep them at my mom's house. After a few days, she would get mad and annoyed with my boys, saying on more than one occasion, "Come get these damn kids or else I'ma send them home in a cab." I would leave every other week and be gone for a few days. Yes, my mother knew all about my boosting. She would say, "I don't know what you're doing, but whatever you're doing, you better do it good." I would as vaguely as possible just tell her that, "I'm going out of town." Mom didn't like that.

Boosting was my lifestyle for years, and it began at about the same time that I got with West Coast, while I was about 23. Boosting was my 9-to-5. After a day's worth of work, I would have snagged $10,000 worth of merchandise. The risk of getting caught was well worth it because we were racking up some money by selling all the clothes for a third of what they were worth.

But I was trained so well that I never would get found out. Or so I thought. I remember the first time that I got busted. The judge gave me 60 days in jail. I had never been incarcerated before, so you can imagine how scared and ashamed I was. Thinking about leaving my sons alone caused a steady stream of tears to run down my cheeks. But that didn't mean anything to the judge. I'll never forget his parting words to me: "I don't know what you're crying for. You're a professional."

He was right about that. With tons of dough coming in from our business, Rita and I would go to Houston, Memphis and Miami. Every week it would be a new city or town. Me and my girl went into a boutique out in the suburbs of Detroit. They had these lush, suede outfits. They cost about $500. Seeing the potential street value, we each put one set in our girdles. But Rita got greedy and decided to slip one of the outfits one in my purse. Our cover was blown when the salesperson saw it hanging out of the purse and called the police. It was until hours later when we were escorted from the police station and placed in the jail that they found out I had the suede outfit tucked into my girdle. The guards told me to strip naked -- which caused another meltdown -- and it appeared out of thin air. "Oh, you got another one," one of the guards said facetiously.

I didn't know what I was going to do. Rita didn't do time because she never showed up for her court date. She had many warrants out for her arrest and more aliases than I could count on both hands. West Coast didn't like Rita because she had a reputation for knocking over all the stores in Detroit, so much so that we couldn't even set foot in any of them, lest we be found out.

West Coast came to see me every Sunday when I was locked up. One time, he brought my kids but they didn't come in to visit. I don't know why but I think they wouldn't let them in. I looked out of the window and saw them in the car, and I cried. I missed my boys so badly. While I was in jail, I caught pneumonia. I needed a sweater so West Coast had his woman named Kim go and buy me one and he brought it to me.

I was released on the Fourth of July and West Coast came to pick me up with his good friend, Johnny Good, who was a big dope man. He was found dead years later, in a trunk of a car with his penis cut off and stuck in his mouth. That day they came to get me, West Coast was in the parking lot of the jail because he couldn't come in and give his name because the Feds were looking for him. This is real deep now! I got out of jail, picked up my kids from my mother's house and his son, Leon, from his mother, and Leon's sister who was staying with West Coast's sister.

West Coast took me to a hotel because he couldn't go home to our house on San Juan, because he was on the Feds' most wanted list. I took a job I had as a secretary at a storage company to support my children. A couple of weeks later, West Coast came back to the house on San Juan while I was at work and the kids were at the house. It was daytime and he was upstairs on the enclosed back porch free-basing. Just like that, the Feds were banging on the door. My son, Carlos, who at the time was 13, answered the door. They asked him if West Coast was there, and he said, "No." They came in anyway and took West Coast -- not to jail, but somewhere I never found out about, and they kept him away for at least seven days. This is when he became a snitch. He told on DC and all 10 of his brothers who had a big organization. After seven days, they let West Coast come home and I asked him where he had been. He gets mad at me for asking, because he never stayed away from home seven days. While he was away, he calls his oldest sister, Annie, and tells her a little something. She found out that he was snitching, so she called me and told me what he was doing and that he was in the fed's company. I said, "Oh, boy."

After I served my time, I went right back to boosting. After many successful trips, I moved on the west side into my own house on Ladder and Fenkell. I let West Coast move in, but soon enough he had turned my home into a dope house -- people coming in and out at all hours of the night, large stacks of cold, hard cash. We stayed there for about a year, until West Coast bought me a real nice two-story house on San Juan, still on the west side. I felt more comfortable about raising my sons at the new place. While living on Ladder, I became a very big-time, international booster and West Coast's status was on the rise to being a very big dope man.

He met a guy named Jim who had heroin connections in Florida. Heroin was black and extremely potent. They had to cut it with lactose because if it were shot in the arm otherwise, it would cause an overdose and death. It was just that powerful. Now that West Coast and Jim had it going on, West Coast one day wanted me to go to Florida to take Jim some dope because his associate was traveling down there. Something happened with Jim's connection in Florida and they all got busted while he was down there. West Coast gave me some drugs to take to Jim down in Florida because he was sick and going through withdrawal from his lack of heroin. I went to the place on Ladder -- my former home turned drug house -- to get the drugs that I would deliver to Jim. Lo and behold, West Coast had one of his new women, Kim, over there lying across the bed. I was so mad at him that I went to the airport in Detroit and head to Florida. When I get there, I called him back and gave him a piece of my mind.

"You dirty muthafucka. Why the fuck you have that bitch layin' all up in my house like she own the damn place?"

"Oh, girl you need to quit." He laughed it off and just acted like I was stupid.

"You ain't shit, nigga. You low-down, dirty dog. Fuck you and that nasty, triflin' trick," I screamed into the receiver.

At this point, people were starting to stare. But I didn't care. That's how mad I was. It was a heated back-and-forth exchange that ended with West Coast Jack telling me how much he needed me and so on. Since I was already there in Florida, I figured I might as well follow through with the plan. I met up with Jim, who wasn't any better than his boy West Coast. He had a girl down there and his wife was back at home in Detroit with his two cute daughters. Jim's wife worked in a factory and he owned a store called 12th Street market.

The next day, Jim took some sherm, a hallucinogenic drug that made him get naked and walk out on the balcony at the hotel he was staying at. The police came; I was on my way to pick up mister low-down dirty West Coast Jack from the airport.

We pulled up to the hotel to a scene of several police cars with flashing lights and a gang of officers. We saw Jim in handcuffs, being placed in a black-and-white and hauled off to the slammer. Now West Coast had a teaspoon of cocaine for his personal use with him, and seeing all the police activity, he gave me his drugs to stash away. My first instinct was to put it in my pocket with the keys to the car. But when the police saw us and escorted us up to the room, I hid the small, plastic pouch of cocaine in my mouth. The next thing I know, we were taken to jail. I was placed in the front seat of the cop car. When we arrived at the police station, I quickly spit the bag out, but my mouth was frozen because of the effects of the drug. The officer asked me for my name, but I couldn't make a sound. West Coast knew what happened, so he butted in and tells him my name is Jazz. He did the rest of the talking at the station. He told the police that we came down from Detroit to visit Jim. Thankfully, the officers saw no threat in us and let us go. They told us to get out of Florida. The next day, they also released Jim and the three of us returned to Detroit.

This whole ordeal was mild in comparison to what I soon would discover about my man, West Coast jack. He was a child molester. I didn't know for years. I went over to Canada to buy him a long, black double-breasted mink coat. While I was away, he went to New York. During that visit, he had sex with his son, Leon's, sister whose name was Ruddy. She wasn't but 13 years old. West Coast had her run away from home and he had his cab driver friend pick her up in New York. Ruddy's mother was a crack head, so the cab driver took the girl to his house, and he and his wife kept Ruddy for a couple of days until West Coast got into the city. He brought that child back to Detroit and she became his woman. Now check this. I come from the two-day Canada trip and go to the house on Ladder. On my bed, who do I see? It's Ruddy. I don't think I had ever seen her before. She was lying with her leg across West Coast's dick.

"What the hell is going on in here?!" I yelled.

"This is Ruddy, Leon's sister," West Coast replied, in an all-too-calm manner. "Her mother put her out and I went to New York to get her."

"She do not have no business layin' on you like that."

The sheer shock of that whole scene blurred my memory of how he responded to me. He said that he wanted me to be a mother to her. I agreed to help her out. I would have loved to not know that West Coast and this child would wind up becoming man and woman when she turned 19. The two of them got their own apartment together in San Antonio, Texas. He put me out.

But back to that day when I had first caught them in the act. I let that go and I didn't think much more about it until about four months later. I was very busy going out of town to boost clothes. I always had Sugar to come over to my house to keep the kids. By now, I had four: Carlos, Lil' Man, Leon and Ruddy. I was crazy about Ruddy because I always wanted a daughter. One day on the weekend, we would always take the kids to my mother and Sugar's house or to his mother and his sister's house so they could give us a break. One day, West Coast went to pick up Ruddy first in a brand-new, white 1973 town car that was in my name -- and then they head to Sugar's house to pick up both of my boys. When West Coast and Ruddy pulled up in front of Sugar's house, they were curled up, holding hands. My sister went off on them.

"Why you got this young baby sitting all up under you and you all holding hands?" Sugar asked West Coast.

Again, West Coast just brushed it off and acted like my sister was the crazy one.

Sugar got my boys ready to leave with West Coast and they get in the back seat of the car. He went to his sister's house to pick up Leon, and they come home to the house on San Juan. By then, Sugar had told me all about it. So when they arrived, I was ready to settle the score.

"What is wrong with you? Why would you be doing this with that girl? You know you're wrong for that. She's old enough to be your daughter. She's just a 13-year-old child with a crush on you, an unhealthy crush at that!"

He didn't say anything in response. He let his firsts do the talking. West Coast threw me to the floor and beat me up really good. He put his knees to my forearms and blackened my eye. Pow! Right in my left eye for what I had said.

A couple of months later, West Coast and Ruddy went back to grandmother's house and she has a boyfriend over there -- Kelvin, a 14-year-old boy from the neighborhood. Ruddy and Kelvin had sex, but kid's sex, where he pulls his pants down and she pulls her panties down. West Coast wanted Ruddy to be my daughter but he didn't tell me that this happened; Ruddy told me. When West Coast finds out about Ruddy and Kelvin, he had her down in our basement on San Juan. He said to Ruddy, "Pull your pants down and show me what you did to Kelvin."

Ruddy came and told me all of this, but I wouldn't say anything to West Coast because the last time I said something, he jacked me up. I was scared to say anything. I knew that other things had happened between West Coast and Ruddy, but they kept it undercover because now all of the family knows. My family, and his family -- even his mother knew he was a child molester.

That wasn't the only thing that was hectic in my life. Two guys who knew West Coast came over to our house on San Juan to rob us. This was on a Sunday that West Coast had been asleep all day. He had a dope selling apartment on the west side of Detroit. He and Cherry had gotten back together after five years, and so Cherry was back selling heroin for him, and was one of his women.

Cherry called the house and asked to speak to West Coast. I told her he was sleep and hung up in her face. A few hours later he wakes up. Cherry called back at about 10 p.m. and brought the robbers to the apartment. She told West Coast that those guys their acquaintances -- wanted to buy a large quantity of drugs, so he got up, put some clothes and drives to the apartment. The guys had been waiting there for him all day. Those thugs robbed him, tied him up and brought him and Sharon back to my house. They rob us, too. When they came into my house, I was upstairs getting ready for bed. The door opens and West Coast, Cherry and the two men come in. West Coast hollers upstairs for me to come downstairs. I put on my robe because I heard voices, so I go downstairs.

"Open your robe," one of the robbers said to me.

"For what?" I replied.

"I said open your robe, bitch." He had a big gun in his hand.

"Baby Girl, open your robe," West Coast pleaded with me.

I did, but I was getting pissed off, wondering what is going on. They all went into the dining room and everyone has a seat. One of the men was standing over this table where West Coast's dope was placed, and right then and there begin to blow it up their noses. Cherry, too.

"What is going on?" I wanted answers.

"Shut the fuck up and pour me a drink."

"You want a drink. Oh, so this is a party now?" I said.

That probably wasn't the best thing to say to the robber. Not fond of my smart mouth, he grabbed me and took me down to the basement.

"Where is the money?" he asked.

"We don't have none."

"You better tell me where the money is. I ain't playin' wit chu."

"What are you going to do, kill me? Well then, you still won't get the money. We spent all the money. Don't you see all this furniture? And I just bought that town car. Don't you see all of this? That is where the money is," I said.

"So you're a smart bitch," the robber replied.

He was looking all around the basement and didn't find anything. He took me upstairs where the kids were asleep. He took a pillow case and put my $250 boots in it and my pants, the clothes I had taken off before I went to bed and a few of West Coast's clothes, too. He looked on the dresser and saw about five or six of my gold chains and took them right in front of my face.

I was really pissed. We went back downstairs with West Coast, the other robber and Cherry. They were still at the dining room table. He put the gold chains in his top left leather jacket pocket.

"Hey, man. What you come up on?" his associated asked.

"Nothing but a few clothes."

I interjected, "He lyin'! He took my gold chains and they're in his pocket."

Man, did the other robber get mad! His partner was holding out on him. I made a very, very big fuss about my chains. I wanted them back, not that they were big chains like West Coast's, but I was still upset. The robbers had West Coast's chains lying on the table with the dope. West Coast got mad at me for cussing about my little chains, but he told the robber that he should just give me back my little chains. The robber said I wasn't getting nothing back. So right in front of the robbers, I went off on West Coast.

"Here you bring these robbers to your home to rob us with this bitch, Cherry."

"Shut up, Baby Girl."

"No, nigga. You shut up!"

By then, the thugs and Cherry were ready to flee. They had taken all of West Coast's money, and as they were leaving out of the door, they said for West Coast and Cherry to go with them and drive them back to their car. West Coast asked the robbers if they would let him keep some money, and one of them turned and threw about 20, one-dollar bills.

West Coast said to me, "Baby Girl, pick that up."

"Muthafucka, you pick it up. You brought these niggas and your bitch in here to rob us. Fuck you."

With that, they left and when West Coast got outside the door, I said, "Don't you bring yoe punk ass back here no more."

"Don't say nothing else to me," West Coast said.

I replied, "Fuck you!" I slammed the door shut and they drove off. About 45 minutes later, there came West Coast knocking on the door, begging me to let him in. At this point, I did, even though I was mad at him and didn't want to talk to him at all. He had dropped Cherry off and he knew I was very upset. I was thinking that his woman Cherry must have set him up to be robbed, but of course he didn't think so. West Coast was real stupid like that. So, he came back in the house on San Juan, went to the upstairs cedar closet, got his mink coat, put it on and left. He also was heated because they robbed him of all of his money, dope and jewelry. They got his rings that he had for every finger, his chains and a watch. They didn't get my really big diamond because I had it hidden.

The very next Sunday, West Coast didn't have any money, so he called home to ask me if I had any. He wanted to buy some cocaine. I told him I did, and he asked me to bring it over to his apartment where he and Cherry were staying. He said he will come down and get it. I got into the town car and go to take him $50, but I stopped at the gas station to fill up. I made the stupid mistake of leaving the keys in the ignition, and a guy hopped in and drove off. A guy at the station had seen everything and tells me to get into his car so we can chase after the thief. We didn't catch him, but the kind man took me home. I called the police and report that my car has been stolen. My purse was in the car with the money I was taking to West Coast. Thankfully, the police found the car a couple of days later parked not too far away from the gas station. And I couldn't wait to pick up my ride.

Back when I went to Canada to buy West Coast that double-breasted mink coat, my girlfriend Emma, who also was a booster, stole a red fox coat. She sold it to me. I needed money, so I went out of town with Rita. While I was gone, West Coast owed some dope man some money, and they came and took both the mink and the red fox coats. Now, West Coast was on the pipe free-basing and he had really gotten strung out. I went to Houston, Texas, and continued boosting. I sent back a big box of clothes that I had stolen, which was worth about $10,000. The clothes arrived at the house via UPS on a Wednesday. I came home on Friday. West Coast was to sell the clothes. When I got home, he didn't have any clothes or my money. I wanted to kill him, but what I didn't know was that he was doing all of this free-basing and that is where all of the money was going. I really didn't know that this man was a real dope head. All of our money was going straight up in smoke for him. I didn't know what's going on with him and Ruddy while I was gone, either. I wasn't focused on that then.

We stayed on San Juan for about three years, until West Coast started losing himself. We ended up losing the house, so we moved to Southfield, Michigan into a two-bedroom apartment, where the boys sleep in the basement. We also lost the Lincoln town car, and I had to pawn my ring for $1,300.

I went out of town boosting to New Orleans with this girl Katrina, who had money orders that I have bought in Detroit for $2. We bought a Paymaster machine and made the money orders into $200. We had no problem cashing them in New Orleans. We went into a store to buy some luggage and Katrina stole a purse. Since it was a luggage store, they only had about five or six purses. I purchased the luggage with this hot money order and when we left the store, the lady missed the purse. She took our license plate number down and called the police, who tracked us to our hotel room. We had a rental car and had been in out there for two days, during which we accrued $100,000 worth of merchandise. When Katrina and I got back to the room, the police were in the room, with guns out. We opened the door and they arrested us and took us to jail in New Orleans. Katrina was talking real smart to them and they told her if she didn't shut up that they would beat the crap out of her. We went to jail and Katrina stayed a week, and then her man got her out. Both of us had $100,000 bonds at first then they went down to $80,000. I stayed in there for 30 days because my man was on crack and didn't have any money to get me out. I needed $10,000-plus to make bail. My mother put our house up after I had stayed 30 days. I guess West Coast was real ashamed, so he and his friend robbed a store near our house in Southfield and he sent the money to my lawyer that I had in New Orleans. His name was Andrew Matthews and he liked me and came to see me every day. The day I got out, Andrew bought my ticket back to Detroit, and I never went back to New Orleans, until I got caught again.

West Coast, he was smoking dope so tough that he began spending time with his baby's momma, Shay. She also had a little house in Southfield that he was dealing dope out of off and on. He couldn't deal cocaine like he used to because he was a heavy dope smoker himself. It was about the time for him to go to prison, and we had an old jeep that we drove since we lost the town car. Little did I know, the jeep was stolen, and I was driving around trying to make money for my family. I got to the airport in Detroit to rent a car and got busted with stolen credit cards. OK, that's a major case I've gotten. To make matters worse, my kids broke into the next door neighbor's house in Southfield, while he and his wife were on vacation. My son Carlos and West Coast's sons, Leon and Jamie, all took the man's belongings and brought them down to the basement of my house where they sleep. The police came to my house and busted them. West Coast was away at prison and they took my son and the others to the Southfield jail. They confiscated the jeep when the found out it was stolen. Carlos, who was about 14, called me from jail, asking me to come and get him. He said it was very cold in there where he was. I was so mad at him that I hung up the phone in his face but I went down and picked him up.

Meanwhile, West Coast was doing his snitching thing real big time behind bars. He got caught up on a parole violation. He even ratted out his boy, D.C. I had to move out of the house in Southfield, and I found a house from a newspaper listing that was located back on San Juan. It was a real nice, big house that was renting for $600 per month. I had West Coast's sister, Valerie, move in with me so she could keep the kids while I went out and hustled money to take care of things. I had a case pending and had to go to court. Luther, our attorney, was there to see about me and they let me go that day. I still had to go back. I had four kids to take care of, and I was taking care of them real well by myself.

Again, in reality, I'm going so fast in the opposite direction that I don't see truly what I'm putting myself and my sons through. What I changed was my sons' chance at a normal life. West Coast destroyed me, and I destroyed them. Can they ever forgive me?

CHAPTER 6:

Abnormal -- Normal

*With the pedal to the metal, Baby Girl was
speeding through life without brakes or steering.
Disaster looms ahead.*

Due to West Coast Jack running his big mouth in prison -- snitching to the Feds -- the government put me and the four kids into the witness protection program, less than a year after West Coast got locked up. I went to jail on another foiled boosting spree, which caused me to lose my house on San Juan. While I was locked up, the children go to their grandmother's house, except for Ruddy, who at the time was in high school.

She moved across the street with her friends' mother. I was in jail myself for about 30 days, when the Feds came and took me to Memphis, Tennessee, and cleared up the case down there that I had run from. They also cleared up the pending cases in Detroit. I had to wait in Georgia for 30 or 40 days because they were putting me in the witness program.

My next destination was to a hotel in Cleveland, Ohio, then all four of the kids, including Ruddy, came up and we reunited. The next day, the FBI brought West Coast. We all stayed in Ohio for the night and the next day they take us to a Holiday Inn in Arizona, and they told us we couldn't make phone calls or let friends or family know where we were because we were in the witness protection program. I definitely didn't want to be in the program, but we didn't have a choice, really. The Feds had to protect us, too, because we were West Coast's family. Carlos and Lil' Man

hated witness protection as much as I did.

We broke all the rules, starting with the one that said we couldn't notify

our relatives concerning our whereabouts. I did the exact opposite of what I

was told. When I found out we were getting shipped away, I immediately got

my mom and sister on the phone. There was no way I could keep something that serious away from them. My family back in Detroit was scared for us, because they knew we were getting into something that we didn't sign up for. West Coast snitched without my knowing. I didn't even know what the witness protection program was or what you had to do to get in there. I was asking all these questions.

While in the program, the Feds got me a job as a gas station clerk, but that was short-lived. During each shift, I would pocket money from the cash register, and at the end of one month on the job, I had stolen $3,000. The FBI gave me a lie detector test and I passed it. They would ask, "Now, did you take the money?" In my head, I would answer, "Yes." And then in the calmest tone I could conjure up, I would respond, "No." Man, were they hot with me. They had a hunch I was stealing, but my polygraph test

told otherwise. Needless to say, I was fired. After that, I got right back into boosting. San Antonio wasn't used to a booster as professional as me. My kids were no better. They went buck wild and started stealing cars. When we were staying in the hotel, they broke into a man's room and stole all his money. When the police came to question Carlos, he stuck the money in my pants pocket, so they didn't find anything on him. The boys would go into the shoe store, ask the salesperson for five or so different sneakers, and

then grab the stack of boxes and run out of the door. Around them whites and Mexicans, they took anything they could.

The FBI all let us choose new names, so I picked the most Mexican-sounding last name I could think of: Chavez. I thought I might as well be like the rest of those folks around there. We all kept our real first names. Carlos really didn't like having Chavez as his last name. He rebelled at school and would show up with his shirt all open. And most of all, he hated being driven to school by the white men from the FBI.

Now this was when West Coast and Leon's sister, Ruddy, became real lovers. He was going with her big time. She showed me a letter that he had written her while he was in jail and it said, "Ruddy, your ass has really gotten big." That messed me up when I read it -- her being so young and him supposedly being a father figure to her and all -- but I was scared to say anything to him because the last time I spoke up, I got a black eye.

The Feds were paying for everything and they gave West Coast money to feed and clothe us. That was short-lived because as soon as he found a dope house, he started spending all his money on his drug habit. I thought that was pretty bold of him, given that the Feds were basically embedded in our family.

My sons would say things to me about not liking West Coast. At that time, they didn't know that he was physically abusing me or that he was addicted to drugs. They called him Jack -- not once had they called him Daddy. Carlos and Lil' Man had a relationship with their real father, Poppa Swotty, even though he and I separated when Lil' Man was only 6 months old. As the years progressed, their dad kind of lost his mind and lived in a nursing home.

They would see him and spend time with him. Time had gone by so quickly, probably because of how caught up in the fast life West Coast and I had become. New Year's Eve crept up while we were in Memphis. West Coast snuck next door into Ruddy's room while she was asleep at about 10 p.m. He starts touching on her, and starts screaming when she is woken up. I was in the next room and heard it, and rushed over.

He was in the room and the lights were out. I caught him in the act and he started fighting with me.

"Not again! Why you over here feelin' up on her? She is 17 years old, damn it."

West Coast said nothing but shoved me against the door, reached back and swung his right fist, aiming right at my lip. And then he hurled another punch at my right eye. That's all he ever aimed for.

The two of them left together in a cab and end up staying all night in another motel. They came back to the Holiday Inn, where we were the next day at about 3 p.m. West Coast and Ruddy stayed up late playing backgammon every single night. I told him that she had to go, but West Coast insisted that she wasn't going anywhere. He and Ruddy were having sex almost nightly. All the things that West Coast and I were supposed to be doing as longtime boyfriend and girlfriend, he and she were doing.

It was an unfortunate scenario that I got used to after a while. West Coast would leave the house. Then, five minutes later, Ruddy would sneak out. Lil' Man would go through the bushes and watch her get in his car, while I was cooking. Lil' Man would tell me, and they'd be gone for 30 minutes and come back in the house, as if nothing had happened. If I said anything, I would pay for it with a busted lip or a black eye. I was scared to leave. This one time, West Coast took a large red ashtray and smashed it. With a crazy look in his eyes, he picked up one of the shards and put it within centimeters of my cheek, and said, "I'll cut you, with yoe pretty face."

Still in the witness protection program, we all moved into an apartment. They would hang out all the time at the swimming pool in the complex. West Coast was in love with her. He even got Ruddy pregnant, but she had an abortion. They put me out and the two of them lived together in the apartment. I was devastated. I didn't think that West Coast would ever do something like that to me.

I ended up staying with a female friend, Rachel, a white girl I met a while back. She lived in Mississippi and she took me in to live with her and her daughters, and I would cook for them. I basically was their housekeeper. I remember this one time, I outdid myself in the kitchen. I decided I wanted to cook a whole turkey, just to say I did it. I seasoned it with some sage, salt and black pepper, and coated it on the outside with butter and put four sticks of butter inside the turkey. That's where all the flavor was. I tell ya, that was the prettiest turkey ever cooked in my life. The crazy thing was, after all that drama, West Coast still wanted me -- and I wanted him -- but he and Ruddy were still in the witness program and they had a two-bedroom apartment for just them. I couldn't go there, but one day he let me into their place to spend the night. Ruddy got mad at me and was upset because West Coast was letting me sleep in their love shack. She got mad at him and told him to put me out and he did. I left my leather pants there and Ruddy threw them away, that spiteful little bitch. Now Ruddy was so in love with him that no longer was I her stepmother. I was her competition. West Coast was the same age as me, 26 years old. I was sick of him. We weren't married, so it had been time for this nonsense to change.

The Feds knew what was going on between Ruddy and West Coast because I would call them to come over, but they said there was nothing they could do because she was 18 by then. But I knew there was something I could do. When I had about enough, I had packed my bags and was ready to show out to get my point across. I was out on the front lawn of the house cussing up a storm for the whole neighborhood to see and here.

"This muthafucka fuckin' this bitch who supposed to be his daughter. That bastard been fuckin' her since she was 13. I'm ready to get up out of this shit."

"Ma'am, please lower your voice. You're causing a scene," one of the FBI agents said.

"Naw, fuck that. I ain't lowerin' shit -- not when this muthafucka is fuckin' this bitch! Y'all getting' me the fuck up outta here. I know that much."

"All right, ma'am. We'll let you out, but please keep your voice down."

The Feds pulled out an envelope and gave me $1,900. Just like that, me and my boys were out of the witness protection program. I left because I knew the FBI would protect me as I made my escape. I had my way I wasn't scared that day. If it weren't for the FBI, I would have never gone.

It seemed like we were in the program for years, but it had only been a few months. West Coast ended up staying for about two years. I left with my two sons and went to California to live with my sister, Tulum, and my niece and nephews. We were ready for a new beginning with our freedom intact. I flew out to California, while, Carlos, who was 14 at the time, and Lil' Man, about 9, rode the Greyhound.

I was enjoying the change of pace of being out in California. Without all that drama, I started to regain a sense of what normal truly was. Maybe I could move on and meet a man who could give himself completely to me, someone who could be a good role model for my boys. Maybe I could get a job that paid well and re-establish everything that West Coast single-handedly had destroyed with his drug and sex addiction. Maybe I could have a nice three-bedroom house and a decent town car. These ideas were fleeting. I wish

I had started working toward making these hopes and aspirations become a reality. Instead, I was slow to get on my feet. It had only been but three weeks that my boys and I were out that way, and West Coast was calling me, trying to get me to come back to him.

"You know I love you. I need you back here with me," he said.

"The Feds ain't gonna let me just come back to Memphis to join the program like that. I think that's a long shot."

"Oh yes they will. I'ma tell 'em that some of those cats I snitched on had seen you out in Cali. They ain't just gon' let you be an open target like that."

"All right. We'll see if they buy that," I said, unconvinced that they would.

Apparently, they did, though, because the next day or so, West Coast called me back with the news. I could come back into the program but they were not going to pay my way back to Massachusetts. I was ready to go back to West Coast, but my son, Carlos, who then was 16, said he wasn't going back with me. He didn't like the way West Coast treated me and hated living under the confines of the government at all times. I told Carlos that didn't have a say in the matter and he ran away from home. My youngest son, Lil' Man, didn't want to go back either, but I took him to Memphis with me anyway.

Right away, it was the same ol' same. According to Leon, while we were gone for about a month, West Coast and Ruddy were sleeping in the same bed together. This was the bed that he and I had been sleeping in. Ruddy was pissed because, of course, she didn't want me back with West Coast. But she didn't get it -- she wasn't enough for him because he always had to have more than one woman at any given time. That's how it always had been, and at that rate, I was sure that's how it always would be.

The whole time he was in the witness protection program, West Coast was messing with young girls, including Ruddy and her friends. He'd lick all over their pussies and have real sex with them. Ruddy's girlfriend, Jillie, had sex with West Coast and she was only 17 years old. He turned Ruddy out and screwed her friend Kathy, too, and she was only 16. West Coast would always wind up having sex with the young girlfriends of his son Leon and my son, Carlos He was just ruthless.

A few days after we returned to the program, West Coast and I got into it and he busted my lip and blackened my eye, yet again. His mood changed, and while he was glad that I was back with him, he was even more angered that I up and went to California. I couldn't believe this molester was doing this. West Coast knew what he was doing. He had been a child molester for years.

The Feds moved us from Memphis to Mississippi. West Coast and Ruddy still were going strong. She hated me so bad that one day she picked up a big rock while I was sitting in the chair at our other house and busted me in the back of my head. I jumped up to kick her ass, but West Coast and Leon stopped me and separated us. I was so mad that I waited in my bedroom for about an hour. At the time, West Coast was trying to cut hair for a living and was going to barber school. His barber kit was in the bedroom with me,

and the wheels of retaliation started turning. I got the scissors out then went into Ruddy's room and stabbed her in the arm. I was aiming at her face but she threw up her arms to block the scissors. West Coast rushed her to the hospital. He was very upset with me for stabbing her. At the hospital, they put a few stitches in her arm. West Coast and Ruddy both hated me and ended up staying the night at a hotel. They did that quite a few times. She was 18 years old by then and working at Burger King.

Ruddy and I were getting into it about West Coast another time, then she moved out into her own an apartment, still in the witness program. Things got violent again when West Coast brought me into Ruddy's house. Like a broken record, we were fighting, and West Coast turned on me and kicked me out. They call the police, who tell me to leave because my name wasn't on the lease.

"Well, fuck 'em," I thought. I left to stay with my friend, Joan, in Mississippi, who told me that he was "one dirty muthafucka" who wasn't deserving of me. I told Joan that I was going to move to California with my sister, Tulum, and I did. I sent Carlos and Lil' Man to stay with my mother back in Detroit. I felt that they needed more stability, and my mom should be the one to provide it to them. I moved in with Tulum and her six children, as they were being evicted from their apartment.

I know we had to do something, so I went to my niece, Jazz, and told her to introduce me to a dope man so I could make some money by slangin'. She took me over to this dope house where a man named Nate was in charge, and I waited in the car. He said he wasn't interested in meeting anybody that Jazz knows, including her aunt. You see, Jazz was far from an angel. She would do all kinds of shady stuff, like lying and saying she'd been robbed. Jazz tried to convince Nate that I wasn't trouble, but he didn't want

anything to do with her. She started to leave and he called her back because he changed his mind about meeting me. I went upstairs to prove myself to this Nate guy.

"My family and me, we're getting put out of our place," I explained. "We don't have any money at all, and so I need some work."

After taking a step back, looking me up and down, he peered into my eyes and said to me, "I'm going to trust you, but if you mess my money up, I'm going to mess your life up."

"My word is my bond. You don't have to worry about that," I told him.

Nate gave me $1,000 worth of rock cocaine. I took it down in the rough area of Los Angeles called "The Jungle" on a street called Coco at 11 on a Sunday morning. By 12 midnight, I'd sold every last one of those rocks, just by standing on that street corner. It was easier than I thought. I made $1,000 exactly and I took the cash back to Nate. He couldn't believe it. I told him that I didn't have anywhere to stay and he allowed me to stay at his place.

"This apartment is your apartment, but you can't let any of your family members come here," Nate said, handing me the key. "Don't let anyone in."

"I understand. Thanks, man." I said.

The apartment was one where Nate and two of his boys, Preston and Stan, kept their dope and cooked it up. I liked Preston for myself. He was cute with a nice build. Seeing how Ruddy and West Coast still were living together in their apartment in Mississippi, I knew I could get mine. Nate put me in a spot to sell dope and Stan was the runner. Every time I ran out of my supply, he would bring me more. I started to really like Preston. We were spending an awful lot of time together, and I think things are headed in the right direction with us. Preston and I were kickin' it and one day, when West Coast called me and informed me that he and Ruddy had to give up the apartment because he needed to go back to Detroit and testify against DC and his organization. The Feds gave Ruddy money to get herself a place. West Coast showed up to court in Detroit wearing a long-hair wig and glasses, trying to disguise himself. He squealed about everything he had on DC and a whole lot of other people, including his attorney.

After he did that, West Coast and DC's brothers and cousin got sentenced to some serious prison time. They didn't catch DC and they were searching for him for a long time. The Feds moved West Coast back to Ohio to a halfway house. He stayed there six months then he called me out in California, telling me that he was through with the Feds and asking if I would come back and be with him. West Coast said he loved me and wanted me back. I stayed in California another few months, then flew to Ohio to be with him. I lived in a hotel while he was staying in the halfway house.

Back in Detroit, all of the pimps and players, dope men and hustlers were talking about West Coast Jack and how he snitched everybody out. They called him all kind of names, but they didn't seem to know that he was a child molester while he was in the witness protection program. West Coast befriended another guy in the halfway house and then started going with the guy's young sister, which wasn't unusual. He would introduce the teenage girls to oral sex and they would fall deeply in love with him. My, have times have changed. I remember when West Coast was a big dope man. He never did anything for his family, not even his mother. She lived on the east side in the ghetto, and his brothers and sisters didn't have much, either. West Coast was the only one with money, cars, houses and clothes, and he didn't share a thing with any of them. He didn't buy his mother a nice house like all of the other big dope men did. His friend, Jeff Crawley, was a much better man than West Coast. They were partners, but Jeff actually cared about people. Jeff bought his mother a couple of houses and his brothers, too. All West Coast did was do nasty things with young girls. He was such a sick man.

By then, we had all of our kids -- Carlos, Lil' Man and Leon -- and moved to Ohio. Ruddy was living in Mississippi. She and West Coast were done. She didn't want to see him anymore. West Coast didn't want to go back to Detroit, so we were trying to become a family again out in Ohio. But I knew that this family man side of West Coast would be brief. He was never a one-woman type of man. West Coast soon began messing around with a white woman. At least she was of age. They went together for about six months.

My kids were really getting messed up in the head with all of this. Carlos went to a 7-Eleven store in Ohio and told the store clerk to give him a money order. When the cashier reached under the counter to give it to him, he snatched the whole box from the guy and ran out of the store and gave them all to me. I went out and bought a Paymaster machine and printed them all out for $300 each. I went out and cashed every last one of them. West Coast was working for the shipyard and he would earn $300 at a time. He'd be gone on the ships for long periods of time, and while he was away, I fell in

love with a guy named Ammon.

We met when I was hanging out in the streets, around this neighborhood called Studlewood. He was checking me out, so he struck up a conversation. And we started a business deal. Ammon would buy all the clothes I stole and re-sale them. I still was doing my thing with the money orders, too, to make some extra money. Lil' Man liked Ammon, unlike West Coast Jack. My sons liked seeing us together, laughing and talking. Ammon was tall and brown-skinned with good hair and a thick mustache. He was a real handsome guy who treated me really well. I really liked him but I also still loved

West Coast. My so-called girlfriend, Bernadette, went out and had sex with West Coast and told him I was messing around with Ammon. West Coast got mad and slapped me around in the face with his shoe then twisted and broke my leg. I left West Coast and moved in with Ammon. My son, Carlos, had left Ohio and went to California. Leon had gone back to Detroit so that left West Coast by himself. He was still fooling around with the white woman.

Lil' Man Becomes Big Man

Baby Girl didn't know it but there was a monster inside of Lil' Man, but his monster had the brains of a genius. He also loved women, was an artist, a poet, a songwriter and a jack of all trades. He loved Baby Girl to death, loved his Aunt Sugar like a mother, but him and his grandma, they were one in the same -- same traits, personality. Sulene would always be Lil' Man's encouragement or his backbone when others wouldn't. Until the day she died, she would say, "That was my baby. I held him on my bosom and he would just cry and cry." She would say stuff like, "Here, this my last $100 bill but I need this back. I gotta pay my doctor's bill. And don't you tell nobody where it came from." His grandma told him, "Lil' Man, you go out there to California and be somebody now."

She was the only person besides his dad, Baby Girl, big brother and Sugar who understood Lil' Man. Sulene knew him the most because she taught him the most. She would say, "I'ma teach you how to cook, clean, sew, shoot, hunt, iron -- everything -- because these heffas don't know shit." It was his grandma who taught Lil' Man how to make liquor. Most of the things in life he learned from women but these weren't your average women. He learned how to fight from his big brother, Carlos, but they both learned how to kick ass from Aunt Sugar, a 4-foot-tall ex-Black Panther.

No matter what conclusion you've drawn about Baby Girl, at the end of the day, she looked the best, wore the best, drove the best, ate the best and lived the best.

Now, Lil' Man, since he was about 3 or 4 years old, internally hated West Coast Jackass. He somehow tricked Carlos into liking him, but Lil' Man always plotted to kill West Coast but never did because Baby Girl loved him so much. Lil' Man's first assault on his mom's boyfriend was the spring of 1979, when the family was living on Tuller Road.

For some reason, Lil' Man thought he was the cat's meow -- as Sulene used to say. A classmate suggested that he had good hair and should put a lot of grease in it to make it look like he had finger waves. Lil' Man, being as impressionable as he was, tried it as soon as he got home and ran back outside to impress the girl down the street, as he was wearing his dress shoes, rayon shirt and Swedish-knit slacks -- his 3-foot-tall, long, slick

hair ass. He didn't cut his hair until he was 10. Lil' Man was stylin' and profilin' and the pretty young thang was eating it all up.

Then, there came West Coast to put an end to the fun: "Lil' Man, get yoe ass in here and get that grease out yoe head." West Coast was little in stature but had a way of sounding big.

Lil' Man was embarrassed and said to his friends, "Fuck that nigga. He ain't my daddy."

He just played it cool and kept talking to the girl. West Coast came and picked Lil' Man up and started combing the grease out with a fine-toothed comb. He took him into the house and continued, all the while talking shit in front of his rich, doped-up musician buddy. Lil' Man thought West Coast was jealous because he had nappy hair and always used perms that didn't work.

Now Lil' Man was really humiliated thinking about the kids laughing at him. He took a swing at West Coast, but he didn't get any hits in. West Coast put Lil' Man in his room

West Coast's whole career being involved with Baby Girl, he never hit Lil' Man but once or twice, but he beat the shit out of everybody else. Lil' Man, even as a child, had a look like, "If you put your hands on me, I'm gonna kill you while you sleep, bitch."

Lil' Man hated West Coast's son, too, but Baby Girl was so loyal that she took care of his kids. He was 12 and West Coast's son was 17 -- the same age as his older brother, Carlos, who already had left Ohio. The son pulled a knife on Baby Girl and Lil' Man turned into Superman. He kicked the knife out his hand, socked him in the mouth and he fell under the dining room table. By then Lil' Man was on him like a pit bull on a steak and he was screaming for mercy: "Baby Girl, Baby Girl! Get him off me!"

Several years later, they were in Los Angeles living on 39th Street. Lil' Man, 17 at the time, was watching TV with his girlfriend while Baby Girl and West Coast Jack were arguing in the bedroom. Lil' Man's cousin Jazz and Tito were staying with them, so he takes them into his room to wait. Then, Lil' Man grabbed the iron, wrapped the chord around his wrist and turned the iron upside down so he could stab West Coast with the point.

"Look, I'm tired of this punk-ass nigga hitting on my momma," Lil' Man said. "Y'all jump on his back. I'ma hit 'em in the head with this iron and we can bury him in the backyard."

Jazz and Tito both were from Detroit and twice Lil' Man's age. Tito was one of them off the chain types who would leave bloody animals in your bed. He was a very complicated individual. I just knew they were with the business for their aunt, Baby Girl. But they looked at Lil' Man like a deer in the headlights and said, "Uh uh. You crazy," and walked out. Lil' Man made a mental note: "I'm puttin' they asses out as soon as this over."

West Coast hadn't yet hit Baby Girl, but Lil' Man was committed to fucking him up. "Don't nobody talk to my momma like that," Lil' Man thought. Then the door busted open and West Coast had Baby Girl in the air, carrying her to the couch as she was screaming and swinging. Meanwhile, Lil' Man's girlfriend and his cousins were looking around to see what would happen next.

Lil' Man said to himself, "What now, tough guy?" Before he could say the words aloud, Lil' Man knocked a spark out of West Coast's ass. He hit him so hard that he stumbled. West Coast let Baby Girl go. In shock, Baby Girl left and said she was going to work. And all hell broke loose after that.

Everybody was amazed that Lil' Man hit that chump. West Coast shook it off

and said, "You know you fucked up, right?"

Amongst other things Lil' Man inherited from his mother, Baby Girl, was that mouth. He fired back, "Fuck you, nigga. I ain't fucked up nothin' but I'm 'bout to fuck you up. Fuck all this talkin.' Come on wit it." Lil' Man gave him so many punches that he was almost out, but West Coast used his grown-man strength to rush Lil' Man to the other part of the couch positioned across the room. Lil' Man, being just a boy himself, overpowered having flashbacks of when we was shot. He could see death in the drug-crazed Jackass' eyes. He had seen him kill before so many times in Detroit but Lil' Man knew a bigger, better killer. So as West Coast was grabbing a heavy, thick, expensive crystal, square, long-stem bourbon glass. He broke the bottom on the wall, exposing a fresh, crisp, sharp stem with one hand in the air with the weapon aimed and the other hand on Lil' Man's neck and his knees on his chest. Jazz an Tito were in the background looking like they

would help West Coast if he commanded. As the devil prepared to slaughter the lamb, Lil' Man closed his eyes, grabbed West Coast's belt straps and collar and called silently on the bigger killer: "Get this nigga off me, Jesus." And as Lil' Man stood up to his feet unscathed with West Coast over his head in the air, he momentarily embellished his God-given power and looked around in an instant, and saw amazement on the coward cousins. West Coast commanded, "Put me down." West Coast may have been better with verbal

control but Lil' Man was better with intelligence and sarcasm, so Lil' Man replied, "I'ma put you down," and threw West Coast from the living room to the end of the dining room.

West Coast was hurt physically, spiritually and mentally. He got up and scurried like a rat out of the house through the kitchen. Lil' Man tasted victory. He wished his big brother, Carlos, could have seen it, but just as a spectator. For Carlos would have stolen the show. Lil' Man started parading around the house talking all kinds of mess: "Fuck that nigga. I'm tired of that nigga hittin' on my momma. But I gotta save my strength. I know this. Bitch-ass nigga 'round here licking his wounds."

"He listenin' and he coming back," Tito said.

Lil' Man continued with his onslaught of character assassinations of West Coast Jackass while strategically placing his back against the wall between the six-chair, glass dining table and the huge mahogany and glass cabinet, fully stocked with over expensive china. (This stuff all was too big for the house, but that was Baby Girl's trademark, even 'til this day: Bigger is better. She got that mentality from her mother, 'cause when it came to medicine, she would say, "If one will do good, all of them will do a lot of good.")

Lil Man still was carrying on: "And he ain't never did shit for us." And guess who reared his ugly head. West Coast Jack.

"Man, I ain't never been nothing but a father to you," West Coast said, creeping up like a snake with one hand behind his back.

Lil' Man knew West Coast had something.

"I'ma fuck you up bad this time," Lil' Man retorted. "You ain't show us shit but dope, murder, the streets and bullshit. My brother in the pen right now 'cuz of yoe punk ass. My whole family on dope. I'm supposed to be in college but I'm on dope. You fucked our names up. You had us in witness protection."

This did it: "And you ain't shit but a snitch," Lil' Man snapped.

Wham. West Coast stabbed Lil' Man, but he didn't feel it -- all glory to God. God didn't save Lil' Man's life from being shot down in the streets to be subjected to a demise at the hands of that clown. Lil' Man picked up the chair he already had his eye on and smacked West Coast in the face with it. It didn't end there. Lil' Man slammed him into the china cabinet, shattering everything inside like in a Steven Seagal movie. This dance lasted for 15 to 20 minutes. Lil' Man was knocking West Coast out and then waking him up. He

learned his lesson that day. Lil' Man didn't stop wailing on West Coast until Tito called the police. When they showed up, Lil' Man ran.

When my son should've been someone taking college finals, there he was fighting for his own life and fighting to get me out of a lifestyle I put him in. I'm so sorry for this, so sorry. Words cannot describe my guilt.

Chapter 7:

Locked Up and Escape

Baby Girl was making enough money to keep the household temporarily happy, then has to survive in prison.

As if I needed any more problems to come my way, I cashed the last money order that I had doctored up with the Paymaster machine and ended up going to jail. The police in Ohio came to my house, woke me up out of bed and took me to jail. I got out on bond and left Ohio. My mother had sent for Lil' Man while I was in jail. He was about 12 years old at the time. I moved in with my niece, Jazz, in Inglewood, California. Shortly afterward, West Coast Jack came out that way to be with me. We got a place in the same complex as my niece.

From the onset, he tried to control everything, but I was the breadwinner. I was making good money writing fraudulent checks. I had all kinds of different people's checks. I also would buy stuff out of stores, take orders from people and sell stuff to them at half price. West Coast was on crack so bad that in order for him to keep up with his habit, I gave him half of my money. As soon as I gave him some cash, he would spend it and come back begging for even more.

I helped Jazz with her two girls and cooked for them every day while their mother went out dancing and to the clubs. Soon, all kinds of gang bangers started moving in to the apartment complex and selling all kinds of drugs. Even the apartment manager was on crack. My sister, Tulum, was living downstairs at the same complex. Jazz's apartment was across from me and we all lived in the same building for about a year. West Coast and the gang bangers bumped heads, and it all erupted in a fight that ending with him shooting at them. There was so much drama in the apartment building, although everyone in the building -- including the kids -- liked me and called me Auntie. I did a lot of business with them, as I would get them what they wanted from the stores for half price. Every day, West Coast had orders for tennis shoes, jeans, household goods, floor tiles and anything else people might have wanted from a store. I would get the stuff and he would sell it for drugs.

But that didn't sit too well with me. I got so mad because I wanted money, not narcotics. Drugs can't pay for bills, food, gas and the basic necessities of life. I got my own people and got paid money for the things. Still, West Coast wanted half of the money and I had to give it to him or he would beat me up and take it. My sister and niece both were afraid of him. We all knew that he was a monster -- an ugly beast that I could not escape.

One day, we were at the apartment. I was drinking some wine and the lights had been turned off because we couldn't pay the bill. Me, Tulum and Jazz were burning candles to get a little light in the place. I was drunk and I said to West Coast, "Nigga, you ain't shit. You don't pay no bills here -- you don't pay nothing." He jumped on me and blackened my eye. But I -- assisted by my sister and niece -- tackled him and we beat his ass. West

Coast left and come back when things had calmed down a couple of hours later.

We had a friend, Desiree, who would come over every weekend to hang out with all of us, but the building was overrun with crime and bad characters. Once, when Desiree came inside the gate of our complex, the gang bangers robbed her and kicked her in the ribs. She took her money and threw it to distract the robbers, and she ran up the stairs to Jazz's apartment where we were all living.

This big drug dealer called Shawn moved into the building, and man was he as dumb as a doorknob. He sold drugs but he was on sherm, a drug that would cause you to trip out once you smoked it. Shawn liked Jazz. The police would come inside the building all the time looking for Shawn. One day the police raided his apartment, found drugs and took him to jail, along with just about everyone in the building. West Coast and Shawn had become best friends, as they shared a common love of narcotics. Shawn smoked the sherm and weed, while West Coast's drug of choice was crack cocaine. He also was selling sherm. Shawn would take his clothes off outside and he'd be running around naked. That's the effect that sherms had. West Coast still was proving to be a dirty, low-down person. He would go into the apartments of single women in the apartment and have sex with them.

He loved women and wanted them to suck on his private parts. I guess since I wouldn't do that, he went and got it elsewhere. It wasn't long before the police busted our house. At the time, I had an outstanding warrant from Ohio and so they took me to the jail called Sybil Brand Institute for Women. I stayed there 30 days then, they let me go because Ohio couldn't come and get me because I had stayed out of jail for seven years. The apartment manager kept my furniture, so when I got out, Desiree came to pick me up and I lived with her and her mother. I helped her take care of her mother, who was a very sick old lady who stayed in the bed. By then, West Coast was sent to prison for 16 months for spousal abuse. He went to prison three times -- when he blackened my eye -- for spousal abuse. I visited West Coast while he was behind bars. He was happy to see me. I sent him packages in his name and other guys' names.

My two sons were both locked up in prison, with Lil' Man doing eight years for selling drugs to an undercover agent in Hollywood. This was the first time that my youngest was sent to prison. Carlos was doing time for robbery. Of course, both of my boys had seen the way their mother was treated. They hated West Coast, but I loved him. I never wanted to hurt him or fight him back because I was so in love with him.

When West Coast Jack got out of prison, I moved from Desiree's mothers' house and got my own apartment, for West Coast and myself. He stayed in a halfway house for four months, then he moved to my apartment with me. Right away, he was back on crack. He was very controlling. Next, Desiree lost her mother's apartment and the church people came and took Desiree's mother with them. I let Desiree move in with me. She slept on the sofa of my one-bedroom apartment. Then, Jazz and her two daughters got evicted, so I let her move in with me, too. I was next to get put out about two months later. West Coast smoked up all the rent money, so we all moved to a hotel temporarily. I had money stashed, so we stayed at a Best Western for one week.

Jazz's male friend, Walter, had a three-bedroom house in L.A. and he let us all move in. I went out to work writing checks to make money to pay Walter the rent for me and West Coast. It was still the same situation with me being the sole provider. West Coast did not know how to hustle -- rather, he didn't try hard enough to make money -- so I had to give him the money to give to Walter for the rent so it looks like he is doing everything. All he knew was how to sell drugs -- that's it. But I think West Coast had learned his lesson from all the years he spent behind bars for drug possession and soliciting. When he got out of the witness program, his name was changed to Kevin Clyde, which he picked for himself.

While we were living at Walter's house, West Coast would stay there and baby sit my little nieces, Tonya and Gina, while I went out and wrote checks. Tonya was about 13 and Gina was 5 or 6. One day I came home and West Coast was playing house and make up with the girls. He was letting them put my makeup all over his face and they were sitting on his lap. That just didn't sit right with me. I told Tonya and Gina to go to their room. I walked in and didn't say anything to West Coast, but I was upset -- not with the girls because I know they didn't know what really was going on, but at West Coast because he was trying to start something with them like he did with Ruddy. He caressed her; that's his way of getting comfortable with them. Gina later told me. That was an agonizing ordeal. and to see that the seed already had been planted made my blood boil. Fortunately, West Coast didn't get to Tonya and Gina.

When I was writing all of these different people's checks, I would have their identification and put my picture on top of theirs, then laminate it. I always cashed the checks and I bought my furniture, clothes, food -- everything that I wanted and all of the dope West Coast used. I loved that man so much back in those years that I would do and give him any and everything.

While we were living at Walter's house, my niece was Walter's woman, but she really didn't like him as much as he was into her. After their relationship ended, she moved in with her brother, Ron, in Hollywood. West Coast would get hold of money sometimes. He got a job as a security guard and got paid every two weeks. When he got his first paycheck -- about $600 -- he left and went and stayed with some woman, and they smoked up his whole check. He was gone three whole days. West Coast had no money and only wanted to take a shower and go to bed when he returned home, so my many questions were left unanswered. He woke up the next morning and started back smoking crack. Seeing him repeat the vicious cycle, I got really angered and we started fighting. He scratched me in my face and I began crying.

"Baby Girl, I'm sorry," West Coast said as he came out of our bedroom. "But you can't be botherin' me while I'm smoking' my stuff. I ain't got but a little left and I wanna smoke it in peace."

There was no sense in arguing with him, so I agreed and left him alone. A few days later, Keith, who was a friend of my nephew, came and drove me to some stores all over Los Angeles so I could write and cash the checks I had. For doing that, I would buy him clothes and tennis shoes, which was all he wanted in return for escorting me around. We got back one afternoon and West Coast accused me and Keith of going with each other. Keith was about 24 years old, and I obviously had no desire to be with him -- I was 35. Now, Keith had never approached me in that way as he was a friend of the family, but West Coast didn't like him because he was nice looking. Still, there was no reasoning with West Coast Jack. He scratched my arm and my face, forming a long scrape.

A few weeks later, we moved from Walter's house and West Coast found an apartment for us, where he was working as a security guard. His boss owned some apartments on Westover Boulevard, and he rented West Coast a one-bedroom place. Me, West Coast and Desiree moved into the apartment. It was the month of December. We moved in on the first, but by December 15, I was sent to jail for writing a bad check at Nordstrom in Paramount.

Because it was Christmastime, security was heavy in the stores and I knew that. I had slowed down and wasn't going out as often, but West Coast wanted some crack and asked me to go out and write some checks. I told him I couldn't because of the risk,

with all the heightened security, but West Coast kept insisting that I go anyway.

"C'mon now, Baby Girl. I need some money. Just go on over to one of them stores and go get me some," he begged.

"Look, I ain't goin' for yoe ass, my mother or anybody else right now," I responded.

In a couple of days, I broke my own rule and went anyway. My first stop was Color Tile, where I bought $500 worth of tile, which I sold. I would take orders. I was with my girlfriend Linda who had kept begging me to take her out so she could get some toys for her kids for Christmas. She had a car, a red and white little bug. We were making our rounds, and our little spree ended at the shoe store. When they saw the fake ID I had, the jig was up because I was noticeably older in real life. The store clerk called security and told them what we had on. Linda and I went and got something to eat. That was the last hot dog I had. After I got busted, I went to jail. From jail, I went straight to prison. I knew what time it was -- I was going to prison. I wasn't going to jail. So, I had to adapt to it. That was the first time I got caught doing illegal activity in California and the judge gave me 24 months. While I was in county jail, West Coast would come and see me once or twice a week. Then, I was shipped off to prison in Northern California. Without having a way to get crack, West Coast took matters into his own hands for a change and started writing fraudulent checks himself. He wasn't as good as I was, though. He hit up Color Tile and got busted. The police had to use a stun gun on him because he was trying to resist arrest.

The judge gave West Coast Jack 18 months. So we both were in jail. We lost all of our clothes and furniture, but Jazz went and got my bed and sofa, which she stored in her apartment. While I was locked up, I went to school and got a certificate to become a beautician. I said to myself, "Now I'm bad -- I can do hair!" I became so good at doing hair behind bars that I had a full appointment book where I would fix 15 to 20 heads a day. I was getting paid big time in food and money. The girls I fixed up would have their family members put money on my books as payment. That sorry man of mine, West Coast didn't know how to fend for himself in prison, so I sent him money off my books to where he was.

After all my run-ins with the law, this one played the most important role in shaping my life from here on out. While I was in prison, I found God. I mean really found him. I would go to every bible study during the week and attend church every Sunday. That was sort of my escape while I was locked up. I wrote and copied the bible all while I was in prison in Live Oaks, up by Sacramento, California. They were cottages that I got to say in because I wasn't a hard-core criminal. With my name being changed, they didn't know about my prior history. When I found God, that is when I found out that I needed to get my life together and never come back to prison. It meant that I would never write another check that didn't belong to me. I got out after serving the full two-year sentence and kept my word.

I didn't go back to jail or prison or write another bad check, or boost or do anything else that I didn't have any business doing. When I was released, I went to a halfway house down on Manchester in Los Angeles, and stayed for four months. West Coast got out of prison a few days before me and he didn't have to go to a halfway house, but he didn't have a place to stay. I called my niece, Jazz, and she allowed him to stay at her place, where she also was letting Desiree stay. Desiree was gay but she was my friend -- we're like sisters. She never hit on me.

I got to the halfway house on a Saturday and that evening West Coast came to visit me. My sister Tulum and her man also came to visit me. There were about 20 people, both men and women, who had gotten out of prison and were sent to the halfway house. West Coast came and he wanted to have sex with me standing up in the visiting room of the house, but there were so many people around on that day. I had on jeans and my coat, but I did some maneuvering to make it work. I pulled my pants down and let him put it in me.

West Coast stayed there at Jazz's apartment, which eventually became his.

Jazz moved into an apartment with her two girls somewhere in Hawthorne, and Desiree moved out with her friend Didi. I was in the halfway house for four months. Meanwhile, West Coast got back on crack, real bad. I told him I was done with him. I quit him while I was in the halfway house and I started liking this guy named Lyle, who also was staying at the house. I didn't really like him but he was something to do.

While I was in Live Oak in prison, I was messing around with my counselor. He and I never had sex but we would be kissing and he would feel all on me. I would go to his office to cut his hair and oh did I almost get into trouble for being in his office because some of the other girls in prison knew he liked me. Mr. Williams would bring me gum and food, and he really liked me. His wife told him to stop letting me cut his hair, and the guards were watching us. Mr. Williams told me that if we got caught, that they would send me to another prison and give me more time on my sentence. But he also told me that he would take care of me if I didn't talk or tell anyone about him. I told him that I wouldn't. Just about two weeks before I would be released, I stopped messing around with Mr. Williams because I wasn't going to do any extra time for him. A week before I got out from prison, they transferred Mr. Williams to work in a men's prison. Yes, those men who work in the women's prisons and guards do mess around with the women prisoners. They have babies by them. It wasn't by force, either. The women took it upon themselves to get into relationships with the male guards and workers.

Speaking again about the halfway house I was in on Century, I had to get a job. West Coast had found work in downtown Los Angeles, where he parked cars to pay rent. His freedom was short-lived, as he went back to prison within three months. He got caught with some drugs in his shirt pocket. When the time came for me to check out of the halfway house, Jazz let me stay with her. I stayed at her apartment for nearly four months. I got a job at Charlie's dance club working as a barmaid and manager over the dancers. I worked there for about 2 1/2 years. I wasn't stealing any of the clubs' money -- I said I had found God and was starting to turn my life around -- but I was making big-time money every night in tips. Men would give me money and some would get really drunk and I would take money from them, sometimes in the hundreds of dollars. You see, I still was a work in progress. Before West Coast went back to prison, his mother died. While he was out, his mother had become really sick and was in and out of the hospital. West Coast was on parole and he asked his parole officer if it was OK for him to go to Detroit to see his mother on her sick bed., and he permitted him to go see about her. But that plan didn't quite get off the ground. West Coast Jack was smoking crack so bad that he could never have gotten the money on his own to get his plane ticket to Detroit.

Ironically, right when West Coast got busted and sent back to jail, his mom died. West Coast wanted me to call his parole officer to ask him to let out to go to his mothers' funeral. The officer told me that his understanding was that West Coast did go to see her while she was still alive, although she had fallen very ill, and that he gave West Coast permission to go. He asked, "What good would it do for him to go now that she had passed away?" The parole officer denied West Coast Jack's request to travel to the funeral. When West Coast received the bad news from jail, he cried so hard. I felt extremely sorry for him. He went back to prison and did about nine months.

By the time that West Coast was released from prison, I was doing real well. I have moved downstairs from my niece, Jazz, and am in my own apartment. I let Desiree come stay with me to help me pay half the rent and she did. Desiree had always worked as a sign painter and did very good work. West Coast, once he got out, began living in a halfway house and, at the time, wanted to become a drug counselor. He stopped using drugs for good and never went back to using drugs or drinking. In 1995, which is the year he stopped using drugs, he did become a drug counselor. West Coast was in the halfway house and needed to do the 12-step program. However, he didn't do them; and now when he went to the halfway house, I went back with him. At this point, I've been with West Coast for nearly 20 years.

Once he got out of the halfway house, West Coast came to live with me at my apartment downstairs from my niece. I was working at the bar making real nice money. Desiree was doing her sign work. We were doing just fine. Desiree and I are paying the rent, buying our food, and we are doing really well. But it didn't take West Coast long to slip back into his old, conniving ways. All he did was use people. He moved back in and didn't pay any rent, and he has the nerve to call himself "pimping."

My son, Lil' Man, is in prison and my son Carlos is in jail, waiting to go to prison. No, it wasn't the first time that both of my boys were incarcerated. But what was about to happen next I was not prepared for.

If you're lost, it's incumbent on you to try and find your way back. Making a decision about which way to go while you're lost can really screw you up and guessing, and lucky if you ever make the right decision. I'm free. I escaped, but my boys didn't.

CHAPTER 8:

230 Years

*This chapter was written by Baby Girl's son--
in his own words, his thoughts and perceptions.
Baby Girl's son is serving the 15ᵗʰ year of a 230-
year prison sentence. She suffered unbelievable
depression, uncontrollable crying, no desire to live
and two heart attacks, which took a heavy toll
on her. Through her own words, as well as those
of her son, the following recounts this harrowing
experience.*

Marcel 24, 1994. Carlos paroled from Calipatria state prison for the fourth time being released from prison. Little did he know the full gravity of the events that were about to transpire. Exiting the Greyhound bus terminal to Los Angeles, Carlos caught a jitney cab to his mother's house on Sixth Avenue and Slauson, located in the notorious Rollen 60's Crip gang territory. He jumped the locked entrance gate to the apartments Baby Girl lived in with West Coast Jack, making a mental note to check for any Crips lingering in the area. For this wouldn't be good if Carlos were caught out of bounds in their hood. The coast was clear as he entered the dimly lit, eerie-looking hallway back to the rear of the complex.

"Baby Girl ain't there," announced some older sista cruising the hallways, as Carlos stood dumbfounded knocking away at the door to the address his mother had written to him from a few months prior.

"What? You know my momma?" Carlos asked the woman with a pitiful, lonesome, lost puppy look on his face. "Where she at?"

"Come with me, baby," she said, leading Carlos around the corner to her spot.

Once inside, she announced to the ol', fat, smoked-out brotha sitting in a chair -- the only piece of furniture in the room, "Charlie, look at Baby Girl son."

"Boy," he said, "you look just like you momma."

As if Carlos hadn't heard that all his life, he said, smiling, "Yeah. So where my momma at?"

"Oh, yo momma in jail," Charlie blurted, as if to kick the living air out of Carlos "And yo father went to jail the other day, too."

The rest of their conversation with Carlos in unison was a blur. All he knew was that he had to leave that place. Calculating his next move, Carlos stopped at a phone booth, where he noticed a late-1980s model Caprice. He busted a right, turned down Eighth Avenue with four gang bangers on the creep all staring at the red prison phone book he held in his hand like an idiot. Carlos was consumed with the slower creepin' crawlin' they were doing, when he saw down the block their brake lights went on. He knew the exact tell-tale signs of what that meant and broke into a trot on up Slauson to Crenshaw, where he boarded the 710 line express to Hollywood.

Then, Carlos considered his situation. As he sat on the bus ride now more of a reality -- unlike the previous thoughts he pondered while on the Greyhound -- set in. He thought, "My momma was never there when I needed her." Although, she was always there when it counted the most. As usual, Carlos would have to make a concerted effort to fend for himself and do for himself what nobody even cared to do, which was to go for what he knew. He started jackin' -- what the people in the hood called "pullin' licks" -- right off the bat the first night in Hollywood. Carlos wanted to stop thinking about his mother, Baby Girl, so he got the one thing he knew that would numb his feelings: cocaine rock. He knew that a plan would be necessary for him to pull that off with his little $200 gate money that the state provide all the parolees.

One, he needed a girl and a room. Two, he wasn't buying no sex. Three, he wasn't into taking it. Carlos spent $100 of the gate money he had left on crack, got a motel room, got a girl and got his lungs full for the night. The next morning when the monster came out, needless to say, it was on like Donkey Kong.

Carlos started pullin' licks for that first week, just to get high, until he came across this haunted house -- this squatter's spot in a mini mansion, located on Los Palmas and Selma. That is where Carlos first met and bumped Kandi, who would completely rearrange his whole overall perception of what it is that consists of a woman's rare essence in the creative life force she possesses as a Mother Earth goddess. For what she taught him in the realms of her entity's existence -- in its interaction with his own on a astral plane -- it's something about life Carlos will take to his grave.

Kandi introduced Carlos full-fledged to the P-game. She was his business partna -- together they made a hella bonafide team. While

Carlos pedaled rocks, she sold herself in the prostitution world up and down Sunset Boulevard. From the start of Carlos's release date on March 24, 1994, up until his arrest on July 21, 1994, he ran rampant the seedy backstreets of Hollywood.

The early morning hours of the night before Carlos's arrest, he had a mythical experience while sitting up in his hotel room getting high. He heard a voice in his mind as clear as day tell him, "Carlos, get up and go to the door and draw your gun." As he approached the door and opened it with his pistol out at the side of his leg -- like his father, Poppa Swotty -- had taught him in his formative years. What he witnessed at 3 a.m. would take the place of his very life was but a segment of the power of God working through the vehicle of his thoughts, in that the psychic abilities that we as intelligent animals possess will forewarn of grave, impending danger. It's up to you to listen to that inner voice of Christ speaking through you. There stood "Twin" from the Grape Street Project Crips, who Carlos had previously robbed at gunpoint, reaching in the backseat of a little Nissan for an AK-47 assault rifle. They had found Carlos on the circuit to which he heard they had put a contract out on his head, from Downtown L.A., MacArthur, Chettrua and Lafayette Park to Hollywood and the Sepulveda Track out in the San Fernando Valley.

Oh, but Carlos wasn't going out like that. Raising his straps, about to spit a few in "Twin's" direction, he noticed a quick retreat. As he looked up, smiled at Carlos and jumped back in the front seat, he told his boy to "pull off!" There's no doubt in Carlos's mind that they had come to kill him. Yet again, Carlos escaped death -- not as part of his plan but God's plan to use him in some miraculous way.

That morning while having breakfast, Carlos sent his crimie "Cowboy" out to get -- Carlos noticed six police cars roll up into the parking lot. Out the back of one of the squad cars jumped this Asian guy who Cowboy kept bringing into Carlos's room to buy dope from him -- to Carlos's objections -- the night before.

"Daman," Carlos said out loud. "Ol' boy must have got jacked up in here last night." Using his better judgment, Carlos slipped out the back door of his motel room and hid the gat in the dumpster. When he returned back to the room, the police and the Asian guy, along with motel security personnel, all approached the door of the room that Carlos occupied.

Opening the door, security announced, "There they are."

"Exit the room," one of the officers demanded with his the rest of the crew's weapons drawn.

Come to find out, they were Metropolitan Transportation Authority officers and Cowboy had robbed the Asian guy the night prior. When they arrested Carlos, the Mid City Police Department, officers Victor and Nash, pulled up into the parking lot, by then surrounded by a mob of pedestrians. In the audience Carlos saw Blue Devil, Twin's cohort, another baller Crip he robbed in Hollywood. Blue Devil had on a hoodie and made several umpire-like hand signals to Carlos, grabbing his crotch, his mouth and cuffing his backs as if to indicate their plot had been successful. Those are the horrific terms of torture they had in store for Carlos

The MTA officers turned Carlos and Cowboy over to the custody of the Mid City P.D. As Carlos sat in the back seat of the patrol car, he heard one of the Mid City officers get on the walkie talkie while opening the trunk to his vehicle and say, "I will transport him over by the railroad tracks and kill him. Where's the .45?

Carlos lost it. If ever the parasympathetic "fight or flight" response mechanism would have kicked in, it was then that somehow with Carlos's kinetic force unjammed the invisible lock on the door and then jumped out, running for dear life -- handcuffed behind his back -- into the arms of all the officers who tackled him, hog-tied him and slung him back into the squad car.

But he wasn't giving up so easily. With his full energy force revved up into a frenzy, Carlos waited the next time until Officer Nash pulled out the lot and broke the plastic ankle restraints, jammed the door latch and jumped out again -- this time from the moving vehicle. They must have had a fit. Officer Nash stopped the cruiser, got out and tackled Carlos, and the rest of the policemen joined in and beat him unmercifully. He was taken to LCMC on a stretcher in an ambulance D.O.A.

The last thing Carlos remembered was the officer reaching his hand up under the sheet over his head to shoot pepper spray in his mouth. Three or four days later, Carlos work up in full restraints on the 13th floor of LCMC -- the prisoner ward -- with a catheter on his penis. The police report read, "The suspect became erratic and started banging his head on the squad car window, and that's how we sustained his injuries."

Ain't that a trip? All in all, the lesson that Carlos learned from that ordeal was that out of all the illicit things he did do -- that he didn't get caught for -- the crime he never committed is what lead him to receive the 230-year -- eight life top sentence -- that he currently is serving.

Misty J. Garcia

Carlos was sitting cuffed to the long table, which acted as a divider from inmates and their attorneys, at the L.A. County Jail Attorney Visiting Room. After visiting with the state-appointed P.I. ?? the courts allocated the ancillary funds provided for inmates -- those fighting their own case -- to hire expert assistance, when in walked into the attorney room Ms. Misty J. Garcia.

First she went to check in but kept staring at Carlos from across the room. She then sat down. She looked over her shoulder back at him and retrieved a novel from her tote bag, and then looked back at him again. One thing Carlos knows is, when a woman gives an indication with her eyes that she's feelin' you. That's your cue to feel free to approach without rejection in store, and approached he did. Carlos told his homie, Dirty Rob, sitting out in the next row over across from her to, "Tell ol' girl to come here." He did and she obliged my request by getting up and making her way over to Carlos's row.

Standing opposite of her, Carlos asked her, "Excuse me, but are you an attorney?"

"But of course," she replied rather pompously. Carlos admired.

"Can I ask you a question?" he began. "If the prosecution fails to disclose exculpatory evidence in a timely manner, isn't she subject to sanction by the court?"

Carlos already knew the answer to the question but posed it as a mere conversation piece. She sat down and explained to Carlos three available remedies and our dialogue took on a personal nature. They began discussing theology and metaphysics and a whole slew of other philosophical topics. Despite his mother's tumultuous lifestyle, Carlos grew up focused on expanding his mind. He always was a quick study who enjoyed learning about vast subjects. Carlos then commented on Misty's ring.

"Oh this old thing?" she responded. "It's amber with mosquito DNA from the dinosaur age."

Before she left, she gave Carlos the number and address to her firm and scribbled her personal home number on the back of the card.

"You can reach me here before 6 p.m. and here at home after 7 p.m.," she informed him as she got up to meet her client.

Carlos went back into the high power 33/3100 unit he was housed at in the L.A. County Men's Central Jail and continued about his daily studies of jurisprudence. The next day, to his astonishment, he hears his name being called over the loud speaker for an attorney visit. Carlos thought to himself, "I ain't got no lawyer." Entering the visiting room, Carlos was shocked to see Attorney Garcia patiently awaiting his arrival.

"Greetings," he greeted her, with an enormous smile broadening his entire face. "So what brings you down? This is so unexpected."

Misty's face contorted in a most grueling snarl, and she conveyed with emphasis as she leaned in closer face to face with Carlos,

"How did you knooooww? How did you know I was a witch? You're so acutely perceptive. No one has ever read me like that."

Carlos had to brace himself to keep his mug intact.

He then responded, "I told you yesterday that you were a witch when I asked you about your ring because, unlike the average deaf, dumb and blind, lost/found, so-called Negro you will encounter up in these stoops here at the belly of the beast, I'm a Five Percenter with true, divine esoteric knowledge, wisdom and understanding of self and I felt the energies emanating in your aura from the minute you walked through the gate. It is the self-fulfillment of our divine prophecy that you would come to me. For I willed it to manifest. Now you can either play games and act all fickle in defiance of what is divinely meant to occur, or you can take heed to your calling and act as the arms, limbs and body to my mind and become my partner in life and help me reach my greatest and ultimately to free myself."

They were engaged, and Misty offered to represent Carlos pro bono in the case before their visit subsided. Needless to say, he was spittin' like a mutha.

At their first regular county jail visit, which was only 20 minutes allotted time for general population inmates (This was one of the many perks and amenities of being housed in the L.A. County Jail, not in general population.), Misty showed up with a little treat for Carlos's eyes, as she unwrapped the long trench coat she donned. Carlos immediately feast his wondering eyes upon her ample breast now being disrobed as she sat at the two-inch thick plexy glass window for their visit.

They spoke their pleasantries and Carlos admired Misty for her so youthful physique.

"I put $20 in your account," she said with a praiseworthy smile written across her face.

"$20? What the fuck I'ma do with $20?" Carlos responded rather arrogantly.

"Well, I was only being considerate as toward your hygiene," Misty said with apparent hurt in her eyes.

"I thought you could buy yourself some cosmetics," she continued in language he could tell she picked up from an inmate somewhere.

"Look, OK. I appreciate your consideration. Thank you," Carlos said. "But these are your instructions when you leave here. I want you to go the bank, withdraw $500 and I'ma have a homeboy contact you. I want you to meet with him and give it to him -- and don't worry. He's not a gangster. I would never place you in contact with anyone who would put your career in jeopardy."

Carlos looked her dead in her eyes and asked, "Do you have a problem with that?"

A second too long Misty paused and then replied, "No. Money is immaterial to me."

Monday when Carlos got his 30-minute tier time, he called Misty to check to see why she hadn't showed up for their scheduled attorney visit with the package that he instructed his homie, Wayne, to seal up and drop off at her office.

"Collect from Ansar. This is a California institution. All calls will be recorded. To accept, press five."

"Misty," Carlos sounded off. "What's hannen? Why you didn't show up today?"

"You're using me," came Misty's response in a whiny voice. Carlos could tell she had been crying.

"You don't love me! You just want me as a mule," she scolded him.

"What?!" Carlos screamed incredulously. "What the hell is a mule?"

"A mule is someone who transports drugs to prison," Misty exclaimed. "Your homeboy told me what was in the envelope."

She went on to say that Carlos didn't respect her if he wanted her to do that. Thinking quickly, Carlos hand to convince Misty of his sincerity with his attraction to her 64-year-old self, well past the courting stage -- or else what they'd established as a relationship was doomed.

"Misty, calm down and listen to me," Carlos began. "Stop insinuating that I'm just using you because I need you to handle business for me. Did Patty Hearst tell Sen. Q he was using her? Look, baby. I told you how these eses be taking off on blacks because they got a green light on Crips. That's why I needed you to bring me the handcuff key. But you lead me to think you was down for the cause when you informed me. Baby, I went to the surplus like you instructed, and when the cashier turned his head, I stole the cuffs."

At this time, Carlos had to make her fully understand the severity of the situation of just why she needed to bring that package -- just that one time. He said he would never ask her again to do it.

Sitting before the honorable Judge Jameson, who was visibly irate with the newly acquired attorney's tardiness, Carlos wondered if would bear the brunt of the judge's anger. Carlos pondered briefly over whether he totally blew the rapport he'd established with Misty, when as in a TV courtroom drama, both doors flung open and in strutted an obviously inebriated Misty. She was totally oblivious to the thickening stares in the courtroom. Carlos noted in her left hand a big manila envelope, which she, amidst the disheartening reprimand of the judge, just so nonchalantly walked up and slammed on the table directly in front of Carlos.

"Oh no this dumb bitch didn't!" Carlos thought to himself.

All eyes in the courtroom -- including the judge, bailiff and the D.A.s -- diverted to the package.

"Ah, your honor," Carlos announced rather assertively, "the defendant is ready to proceed."

Back in the court tank, where attorneys are allowed to consult with their clients, Carlos verbally assaulted Misty's character from behind the grill gate, as he opened the package, pulled down his pants and prepared to go the hoop and keister. Its contents were a half-ounce of rock cocaine and a half-ounce of chronic with no grease (nothing but spit).

"Bitch, are you crazy? Coming in here all drunk and late, and slammin' this shit on the desk like that in front of the fuckin' judge. Have you totally lost your marbles?" Carlos seethed through clenched teeth and grunted at Misty.

"Well, I just thought it was a setup by the D.A. She can't stand me, you know, so I just decided to get drunk and go for it. I was late because the deputies held me at the check-in because there was an alarm," she reasoned with Carlos

"A setup?" Carlos said. "Did you think I would be complicit in some scheme with the D.A.?"

"Well, I brought it, didn't I? Does that answer your question?"

A few months later at Carlos's sentencing, when Misty announced that it was her defendant who she filed marriage papers to be wed to, "Oh hell no!" was the reply from Judge Carl Young. "That's a lawsuit. I'm not going to be party to that action, buddy. Oh, no -- out of the question."

Then the judge asked for the record to reflect those sentiments.

The judge sentenced him to 25 to life. Carlos said, "Fuck you, you blue-eyed devil."

The judge said, "OK then -- 230 years. Court is adjourned."

Misty almost fainted when she heard the judge's ruling, sealed into perpetuity with the banging of the gavel.

Carlos was shipped up state to Delano Reception Center and Misty came every weekend to see him. That was until the prison suspended their visits for 30 days because she got caught giving Carlos a striptease show. Once their visits were reinstated, Misty came up here and there -- missing two weeks at a time. It was in 1997. Misty started complaining to Carlos, "I was watching on '60 Minutes' one of the Melendez brothers was trying to get married, and they said that conjugal visits for lifers were being terminated."

Sho' nuff within a few months of California enacting the non-conjugal visits reform for lifers, Misty shook the spot. It took her a year and one day to send Carlos the trial transcripts he had requested from her on many occasions. She even red-lined his outgoing mail to her. The institution monitored his mail and told Carlos that if he "attempted to make contact with Ms. Garcia, either at home or at work, it would be construed as mail harassment and that merited 18 months in the hole."

After transferring to Tehachapi State Prison, Carlos left all the homies wandering aimlessly like cattle on the yard -- gang bangin' to the Blood Kar. His line was pushing straight up to the law library every single day. Carlos had already learned how to draft and file motions from the Billionaire Club Boy Joe Hun and HB from Venice Shoreline Crips who had committed five 187 counts on his own homeboys and had beat three of them fighting his case in propria persona. Carlos would have to learn how to file a writ habeus corpus for his appeal.

One day while in the facility's law library, learning how to litigate, the O.G., who had been admiring all the nude photos that Carlos showed him from Misty, asked him, "Youngster, do you know what you got goin' on here? This is a civil lawsuit. From what you have been telling me, and I have no reason to believe it's all true from what you've shown me as evidence thus far, son."

The O.G. continued, "This attorney has committed the gravest form of disservice to you as her client. She has not only misrepresented material facts to the court -- in misrepresentation of you as a client during trial -- but she has rendered you ineffective assistance of counsel, due to a conflict of interest posed in her being involved personally with you in a relationship. This is a major violation of her code of ethics of disastrous proportions."

He then gave Carlos several cases to study up on.

"You case sets a precedent," the O.G. said. "There's none in the books quite like it, but you can take these to tailor a civil complaint against this bitch. That's going to get your case reversed."

The man also showed Carlos something in the statute of limitation laws that prompted him to file and litigate for two long years on his own -- a malpractice lawsuit against the now defendant Ms. Misty J. Garcia. And that was that.

There is a one-year statute of limitation for a plaintiff to bring an action against their attorney for malpractice, and that's why it took Misty one year and one day for her to send Carlos his transcripts. But the O.G. also showed Carlos in the books where, according to the Americans with Disabilities Act, there is a four-year tolling period for inmates that doesn't even commence until they're release from incarceration. So when Carlos filed with the courts a civil complaint requesting a trial de novo, upon the prima faci merits of his cause of action, the courts granted it.

After the two-year-long battle with Ms. Garcia's attorney, the pretrial court judge granted Carlos attorney's fees to hire a lawyer to represent him at trial. As the matter was on docket to start trial in 30 days, he was asking for a $150,000 compensatory and $150,000 punitive damages. Yet, after countless phone calls, Carlos could not locate one L.A. attorney who would accept the attorney's fees granted to him by the courts to sue another attorney. He later learned that it was because they all were under the same insurance premium.

So Carlos prepared for trial. He had appeared upon the entire proceeding upon telephonic conference calling at the prison, due to the fact that they felt an inmate of his points level (541 to date) was too high of an escape risk. Just before they started, to Carlos's naiveté of the judicial expertise, Misty's attorney pulled a whammy on him that caught him unprepared. Neither of them showed up and the judge ordered Carlos to "enter default on the defendant." He did, and at the next hearing, they filed a motion to set aside Carlos's default, and the new magistrate granted it and "dismissed the case without prejudice."

Carlos was devastated then understood unequivocally what brothas like Jeronimo Pratt had known all along. The court system could care less about a jailhouse lawyer. If you did not possess the certified credentials of an attorney, then you better perfect your skills and bust you a boss female who wanted to help your black ass.

Obtain your amnesty because prison is a form of modern-day slavery.

Carlos later learned through his momma, Baby Girl, that Misty had appeared on "20/20" with Barbara Walters. Misty took a judge down, had him disbarred for offering her client a reduced sentence for sexual favors. If that ain't the pot calling the kettle black, then I don't know what it is.

I wanted my son to be heard, so this was his and my chapter.

CHAPTER 9:

I Swam to the Edge of the Lava Lake, Then Waded Ashore

Baby Girl's son needed her help and she needed some help, so they had to start from where they were with what they had.

began thinking about my son, who was sentenced to prison for 230 years. I made myself get busy trying to help my son beat this death sentence -- it was a coping mechanism for me. I mean, 230 years may as well be a sentence to death. Carlos, to date, has served 15 years.

I was trying to find out where he was at for about three months, but I couldn't locate him. I called down to one of the courtrooms and talked to the bailiff in the very courtroom that Carlos he got sentenced. Bailiff Jenkins said nonchalantly, "I remember you. You're a nice lady. But, I remember your son -- he's a straight up asshole. His attorney was very emotional --"

"Look, I don't care about all that. I'm trying to find my son," I chimed in.

"Well, you're gonna have to call the California Department of Corrections. Your son is going off to prison."

Click. Hearing that, I was furious. I didn't know if they had killed Carlos or what. How can the legal system not know where a person who evidently had contact with that facility is at for three months?

Then, out of the blue, Carlos called me. You don't even know how relieved I was to know that my baby was alive. My son was 100 percent in my corner and we were pulling together. He began walking me through the steps I should take to help get him out of there.

I was so broken. With both my boys locked up, I felt like I somehow could have been a better mother. There was no way that I could just sit around while my oldest child was serving an unreasonably unjust sentence. I had to do something, so I started where I was with what I had.

One day, I flew my mother and Sugar to California to visit Carlos behind bars, in Sacramento. From there, Tulum rented Sugar and me a car to drive up in. West Coast Jack wouldn't let me drive his car. Well, when Sugar and I finally arrived at the prison, the officials wouldn't let us see Carlos because he was in the infirmary, sick with Valley Fever. I cried all the way from Sacramento back home to Los Angeles.

Now, when I think attorney, I think Johnnie Cochran, the famous lawyer who defended O.J. Simpson, as he stood trial for murder. If O.J. got off scot-free, surely Mr. Cochran could come to the rescue of Carlos, I was convinced.

I asked West Coast if I could borrow his car because I was going to Johnnie Cochran's office, but he told me no because he had something to do. I wasn't going to let that stop me, so I went out and caught the bus. But as soon as I got my foot in the door of his Miracle Mile-area office, I learned that the firm no longer was taking criminal cases -- they were only taking civil trials. I cried my eyes out right there in the office. I guess they felt sorry for me because they referred me to another attorney. I went to him, but he wanted an arm and a leg to take the case.

I came back home and told West Coast and he never said a word. He didn't care, even though he was making a thousand dollars a day and could have put some money up for someone to take the case. After that major setback, I continued my search for a law firm that would take on Carlos's case, only have the next three offices outright refuse to

hear me out. I gained some ground when an attorney from the law offices of Stevens, James & Benjamin LLP agreed to help. He told me he was busy with other trials but ours would be the next case he made a priority as soon as he could. Several months later when that hadn't happened my grueling quest for justice continued. The next lawyer I met said he would take on the case if I put down $2,500. He then decided he didn't want to help me after all, once I shared the details and presented him with transcripts. I even went to

the Internal Affairs Bureau -- they really turned me down. I thought of all people, they would help me.

I continued to call many, many lawyers and none of them would take his case. Money talks and I just didn't have enough of it. I felt so bad because nobody wanted to take his case. They acted like Carlos had killed somebody, yet he only was charged with robbery. They just put him in police lineups, but they never actually caught him robbing anyone.

I sent letters to Oprah's and Montel Williams' talk shows, even to the Bar Association, but didn't get a response from anybody. Further complicating the situation was when Carlos went into the hole for fighting and he couldn't walk me through the process any more.

Throughout the ordeal, I suffered two heart attacks. The first episode happened right after I had chemotherapy for my thyroid disease. I was walking across Broadway and fell out. The last one was in 1998 when I saw the picture of my son all bruised and battered, literally dead on a hospital bed. Thank God the doctors were able to bring Carlos back to life. I brought that very photograph to the Mid-City Division of the Los Angeles Police Department. The officer who spoke with me took the picture and later destroyed it.

Still, I pushed on. I hadn't had any luck yet, but I hadn't given up.

I visit my son as often as I can. Being that Carlos had gotten in a lot of fights, he was shipped around to different correctional facilities throughout the state of California as he serves his sentence. Now, he's in Lancaster.

It pained me to see clearly that West Coast didn't care about my boy. Although, when West Coast when he went to prison, he told me, "When I get out, I'm gonna help Carlos get out."

"How you gonna get him out and you can't keep your own self out?" was my response.

By then, West Coast was a preacher, but he still was cheating on me with other women. Now, he would leave me and his son, Charles there to sell computers and wouldn't pay us one dime, so we stole our money from him but all the money would go into my hands first. I got mine and Charles got his.

My son, Lil' Man, came home from prison after doing eight years. When my son saw me, he didn't like the way that I looked in the aftermath of the heart attacks and my battle with a thyroid disease, which is why I endured radiation. My eyes were really big and looked like they would pop out of my head. My hair had come out really badly and I had lost a lot of weight. West Coast didn't like me anymore because I didn't look good to him. So he cheated on me nonstop.

West Coast was tricking with too many women to name, but he made me stay at home selling computers. Now he had the whole front yard full of computers, and they were selling like hotcakes. He dressed up every day and treated the computer business like a dope business, since he didn't keep any records and kept all of his money in his pocket. He'd have thousands of dollars in his front pocket, just like a pimp. He had no bank account; I mean this man was a trip. I thank God that I am not with him today.

This had hurt me immensely, so badly that I didn't like preachers, as I thought they were all the same: no good. I didn't think that about my pastor, Rev. Witherspoon because he never showed me any dirty acts. He was truly a man of God and one time I went to Rev. Witherspoon to tell him some things about West Coast and how he was doing me. He said that he had an idea that I was being mistreated, and offered to pray for me. His preacher friends would ride in West Coast's SUV that he had just bought and they would listen to worldly music like the Ojay's and Gerald Levert and go out to dinner. West Coast would feed his buddies but not his wife -- me. He never went to buy food from the market, only dog food and coffee or other things that he wanted. One day, he took his friend Ray to dinner and when he left, I was there at the house with the computers. I asked him to bring me back something to eat. His friend Ray reminded him to get me something to eat and he told him he wasn't going to get me anything. He got dinner for himself and Ray and when Ray asked him why he didn't get anything for me to eat he said I was stealing money so I could get my own food. Ray thought that was pretty messed up.

It was a sad state of affairs and all I had left was my son, who is in prison with a 230-year sentence. I knew that I needed to gain focus and the will to fight on, but I was so beat up and tired. I felt like I was dying there and I knew that I needed to get away before I really did. I could only think of one place to go and that was back home to Detroit. My sister,

Sugar, was there, my mother was there and so was my brother, JB. Broken and emotionally battered, I headed back to Detroit.

I didn't think my way out of the hell I was in. I just somehow survived and now, with God-given wisdom, I have turned my life around. I may be scared, but I'm not injured. I could be in prison or even worse -- dead. This could be you. If you find any similarities between my life and yours, stop, back up and take off in another direction. Do this and you will thank yourself later. I dedicated this book and my life to my boys. To them, I say, "Mama loves you always."

CHAPTER 10:

Still on the Planet

Now with a positive influence, Baby Girl has God in her life and now the sky is the limit.

I was in Detroit taking care of my mother. I would take her to church practically every Sunday, and that is how I began to develop a true relationship with God. He knows I needed Him, after all these years of emotional and physical abuse. I also took mom to bible study which, I was teaching and I was teaching Sunday school to children. My sister and I would take my mother back and forth to the hospital, and to her doctor's appointments. We made sure that she kept all of her appointments, as her health was failing.

She passed away at 92, and I was OK with her dying. I knew she had lived a full life and I had my baby sister, Sugar, to get me through. We both, undoubtedly, were there for our mother and that fact helped. I knew my mother was crazy about me, her "Baby Girl." I look back with fondness, remembering that I'd been there for her, even in the snow making sure she got to church. She loved church and would fuss at Sugar to hurry and get her ready for me to pick her up for church.

A month before she passed, I went to my mother and told her I needed to get back to California because I wasn't making any money there in Detroit. She told me to go ahead back because she would be OK there with Sugar. I packed up and got a U-Haul truck and had my brother, JB, help me drive back. I was back in California a month when I got the call that my mother had died. As soon as I got the word, I booked a flight back to Detroit to help Sugar take care of the arrangements to bury our mother. My sister and I went shopping to pick out some clothes for her to be buried in and we got a really special outfit and put her away real nice.

After burying my mother, I stayed in Detroit for a while. I got my truck that I had left there, and me and my cousin drove it back to California. I sent my cousin back home and tried to pick my life up in Los Angeles. I went to see West Coast a few times, but I was pretty well done with him and was ready to wrap it up with him for good.

I was doing all right. It was March 2009 and I bought me a 2010 Mercedes Benz. My sister and I went to visit her son and West Coast, who are both in the same prison. West Coast was very happy that I bought me a Mercedes. He was trying to see it from the yard of the prison, standing on his tip toes and looking out. He was causing somewhat of a scene.

This prisoner, a short, surly white man, asked me, "What he's trying to see?"

West Coast chimed in, "Our Mercedes Benz."

The prisoner looked at my face and said, "Our Mercedes? Are you going to be driving it?"

"I would hope so," West Coast said, copping a serious attitude.

That was my last time seeing him, the man who I inexplicably loved and allowed back into my life time and again. I wasn't going to go back to him. I knew for sure that he still had the same pimp-style attitude and ways. No, I didn't need to see him again, be controlled by him again. Feeling confident and overjoyed by my decision, I talked to Lil' Man one day and told him I wasn't going to go back with West Coast, whom he so hated. Lil' Man just sucked his teeth and said, "Yeah, whatever." I knew that his reply meant he didn't believe me -- and I can't blame him for his disbelief -- so I left it alone.

Sugar, her baby son and my brother, JB, came to visit me from Detroit and were all in the dining room talking. Lil' Man was talking about West Coast and he said to me, "You better not go back to that nigga, West Coast." I got so upset with him because I had told him weeks back that I wasn't going back to that sorry excuse for a human being. It ended up becoming a hot discussion between all of us. Over and over, I said that West Coast and I are done.

JB said, "That nigga ain't comin' back to stay in yoe house -- not while I'm around."

By then, I was really pissed off.

Finally, Lil' Man said, "If that snitching nigga comes back here, I'ma kill him."

That did it. I left the dining room, went to my bedroom and closed the door. Then came

Lil' Man yelling at my door, "The next nigga you get better have the four Cs."

I jumped up and snatched the door open.

"What the hell's that supposed to mean?"

"He better have a career, credit card, company and cash," Lil' Man said, looking me dead in the eye.

I slammed the door in his face. After that, everything calmed down.

Lil' Man ended up getting into some more trouble and went back to prison, getting a new number. He should be getting out soon.

So, West Coast Jack got out of prison on August 6, 2010, after his eight-year stint for knocking a guy's eye out. I chose my new man on August 1, 2010. I hadn't been with a man for seven years. One day, my new man "to be" was in the nail shop getting a manicure and a pedicure. We got to talking. I told him I was from Detroit and he said he was too -- what a coincidence. Rolland said he had nine brothers and one sister. He said their last name was "Luther."

At that point, I got chills.

"I know all of your brothers: Huey, Daryl, Petey, Earl, Marcus, Joseph, Arnel, Nathan and Oscar!"

"Shut up! You sure do know them," Rolland said, shocked at what he had just heard. "You got a man?"

"No, I don't have one and I don't want one."

Rolland didn't say anything. When it was time to leave, he gave me one of his flyers. That night, I called him although, I wasn't interested starting a relationship with him. We were talking and I started telling him about my son who had been sentenced to 230 years. He was shocked and said, "We've got to get him out of there."

He said his cousin was an attorney and that he'd arrange for us to meet to discuss how we could get him out. Sure enough, the next day he called and asked me to meet him after I got off work. I drove to meet him and he was waiting for me at a Hilton Hotel. He was in the lobby where his cousin's office was on the top floor of the Hilton office building. I went in with him to see his cousin "yesterday you told me that you didn't have a man and didn't want one."

"Well, you have one now," and I said, "Alright."

West Coast didn't call me for four weeks.

When he finally did call, he asked, "What's going on, Baby Girl?"

I said, "Well first off, I have a man."

His voice dropped and he said, "Does he treat you better than I did?"

I answered, "Yes, way, way, better. He has treated me better in three weeks than you ever did in 30 years."

He was silent. He couldn't say anything. Finally he said, "Can I call you sometime?"

"No, you can't," I responded and hung up the phone.

Rolland and I were talking about West Coast.

"I'm detecting some fear in you about him."

I didn't reply.

He then said, "Do you need me to talk to the nigga? Because I will."

"No."

"Only you know if I need to talk to tha nigga. Let me know when and if I do, 'cuz you my woman now."

I started feeling a love for him then (not in love with him), just a feeling of love because he showed such care and concern for me.

He wined and dined me all over town. We were having big fun and good times together. Life is good.

Baby Girl's life has been a roller coaster; both up and down, with really high highs and really deep, dark lows. Right now, she is at the high of highs. God is in her life and she's teaching bible classes and working in a health-care environment to help people. I'm studying the word and gaining stronger faith in the Lord. I am ministering to others who are alone and lost; and learning myself along the way.

Baby Girl had quiet before the storm and she was dismantled into broken little pieces. She was misguided into darkness and yes, she lived life in the fast lane. She stole and she was locked up and she saw her son given a "death" sentence. She swam to the edge of the dark, murky, lava lake of life and she waded ashore. She found the Lord, and love and she remained on the planet; beginning to thrive. The sky was now the limit and she would never look down or back again.

About the Author

Tweetie Bond was born on the north end of Detroit, Michigan and is the second youngest of her two brothers and two sisters.

After living in the fast life, experiencing abuse by men for years and surviving several trials, Baby Girl committed her life to God. However, now that many blessings have come her way, she knows that the pain she endured was not in vain. Throughout it all, the joy of her life has been her two sons.

Ever since the dark chapters of her life have closed, Baby Girl has grown immensely. Her hobbies include teaching the nursing home ministry at her church and touching lives with her exuberant personality.

She is free, and for this new lease on life, she has God to thank.